I got

"You know," I explained patiently, "we've done it like a thousand times before at SVMS. We'll switch places."

Jessica still looked dumbfounded. "But—," she said, and stopped. "You hate switching. I always had to beg you to do it."

"I know," I admitted. She was right—I do hate it. "But I want to help."

"So *you* would plan the dance?" Jessica asked doubtfully.

"Sure," I said. "No problem. We'll switch clothes. No one ever has to know. Okay?"

"I don't know," Jessica said, gnawing a cuticle. "You hate dances."

"So? You can give me all your notes—I'll do it just the way you want it," I pleaded.

"Promise?"

"Promise," I assured her.

"Okay, I guess," Jessica agreed reluctantly. "It's not like I'll be going to the dance anyway."

I wasn't sure what I had just gotten myself into, or if I should have let Jessica work a little harder to talk me out of it. But I was committed now.

Don't miss any of the books in SWEET VALLEY JUNIOR HIGH, an exciting series from Bantam Books!

Twin Switch

Written by
Jamie Suzanne

Created by
FRANCINE PASCAL

BANTAM BOOKS
NEW YORK · TORONTO · LONDON · SYDNEY · AUCKLAND

To Diana McNelis

RL 4, 008-012

TWIN SWITCH
A Bantam Book / November 1999

*Sweet Valley Junior High is a trademark of
Francine Pascal.*

Conceived by Francine Pascal.

 Produced by 17th Street Productions,
a division of Daniel Weiss Associates, Inc.
33 West 17th Street, New York, NY 10011.

ISBN: 0-553-48668-3

Published simultaneously in the United States and Canada

PRINTED IN THE UNITED STATES OF AMERICA

OPM   0 9 8 7 6 5 4 3 2 1

Jessica

"Yes!" I exclaimed. "I'll definitely do it!"

My friend Kristin Seltzer stopped walking and turned toward me, her hands on her hips. "But Jessica," she said with a laugh, "you don't even know what I'm asking you yet."

"I don't care. Whatever you need me to do, I'm there," I answered. "I want to be in on whatever's going on at school. I'm tired of being the *new girl*."

Kristin narrowed her bright blue eyes. "So you'll do anything I ask?"

Her voice was serious, but I knew she was joking. Kristin had just been elected Sweet Valley Junior High's eighth-grade class president and was majorly popular. You'd think she'd be really conceited, but Kristin isn't like that—she's the best.

"Well, not *anything*," I disagreed. "But I have a feeling you wouldn't ask me to do something too, too terrible. Right?"

"Why not? You're just a lowly new girl." Kristin

gave me a little bump with her elbow, and we continued walking down the crowded hallway toward the school exit. "Actually," she went on, "it must be hard, starting a new school in the eighth grade, when everyone has their group of friends that they've know since forever."

"It *is*," I insisted. "At SVMS I could have run for class president. But here no one even knows who I am. It's depressing."

I know it sounds kind of stuck-up, but it's true. At Sweet Valley Middle School, I, Jessica Wakefield, was one of the most popular girls in the class. *And* I had a really tight group of the coolest friends—we were inseparable! Plus SVMS only went through the eighth grade, so I would have been part of the ruling class.

But then I was the victim of a terrible tragedy. I was transferred.

I mean, did they *have* to go and rezone the school districts over the summer? Just in time for my last year of middle school? It was totally unfair. Not to mention rude.

SVJH had a ninth grade, so eighth-graders didn't have as much clout. Now I was just some average, semiaccepted new girl. Sure, I had made a couple of friends, but I wasn't part of a really tight group like I was used to.

"At least Elizabeth got transferred with you,"

Kristin pointed out as she pushed open the door and stepped into the sunshine. "That's like having an automatic best friend."

Elizabeth is my sister. Well, not *just* my sister—she's my identical twin.

And Kristin was right. I *was* glad Elizabeth was at Sweet Valley Junior High with me—it made transferring a whole lot easier. But it's not like Elizabeth and I run with the same crowd or anything. Elizabeth is kind of serious and a bookworm. Not my scene at all.

Of course she can be cool when she wants to be, and having her around had definitely made me feel less alone. Even during those times when I was sure I'd never have any friends at SVJH *besides* her.

For some inexplicable reason Elizabeth didn't seem to have nearly as much trouble as I did getting used to our new school. She'd made two fast friends right away—Anna Wang and Salvador del Valle—and started a 'zine with them. My start at SVJH had been a little more . . . rocky.

"Elizabeth is great," I said to Kristin. "But her friends? Please. They're so annoying and uncool. I don't know how she can take them." We jogged down the school steps and headed for my bus stop.

"Agreeing to be on my Homecoming Day poster committee isn't exactly the coolest thing in the world either," Kristin said.

"Sure, it is," I insisted. "You're the chairperson, and you're cool. Cool chairperson equals cool activity."

Kristin smiled and shook her head. "Whatever."

"Kristin, think about it," I pressed on. "You were just elected president! Everyone likes you. You're pretty. You're smart. You're—"

"Pudgy," Kristin cut me off.

I stopped short. "No, you're not," I said.

She shot me a look as if to say, *Give me a break, Jessica.*

"Okay," I relented. "So maybe you're not a stick. But who cares? You *are* pretty."

I meant it. Kristin has great blue eyes and the best wavy light brown hair. I guess she's . . . curvy, but she wears the coolest clothes, and she has a really cute, really sweet boyfriend—Brian Rainey. Well, they're not officially going out, but almost. In fact, when I thought about it, Kristin had just about everything going for her. I was really lucky to have her for a friend.

"So, anyway, would being on the committee mess up your track meets?" Kristin asked, changing the subject.

"No way," I replied. "Track is usually over by four, so I can make posters then. Besides, I'm sick of only doing track. I want to do more school activities

4

and meet more people." Just then my bus pulled up, but I let it go—I could take the next one.

Kristin grinned. "All right, all right. If you're really in, I need four posters by tomorrow morning. Can you handle that?"

"Absolutely. What should they say?" I asked.

"Just the basic information," she said. "We're playing the Redwood Middle School Dolphins at Homecoming three Saturdays from now. The game is at noon. After that, add a lot of team spirit. You know, 'Go, Sweet Valley, go,' and 'Yay, Wildcats,' kind of stuff."

"That sounds easy," I told her. "Anything else?"

"Nope. That's it."

"These are going to be the most amazing posters you've ever seen," I promised. "I am *so* into it."

"Great. Thanks, Jess," Kristin said, turning to go.

"See you tomorrow—with four awesome posters," I called.

Kristin waved. "See ya."

I waited anxiously for the next bus, psyched to get home and work on my posters. I really wanted to do a good job. Being on Kristin's poster committee would mean getting to know more people. Which meant more friends. Which meant *finally* being accepted at SVJH. Which was what I wanted more than anything.

Kristin

As I walked away from Jessica, I felt that familiar worried frown creep across my face.

I wasn't worried about the posters Jessica would make. I knew they'd be awesome because when Jessica does something, she gets completely into it.

It wasn't Jessica I was worried about—it was my friend and sort-of boyfriend, Brian Rainey.

I've had a crush on Brian since sixth grade. He isn't like any other guy in school. He's so laid back, and he's always in a good mood. Nothing seems to bother him.

And he is so cute! Completely adorable. Green eyes and chin-length brown hair, tall and skinny—I get all tingly just thinking about him.

The main thing I love about Brian is that he's so easy to talk to. Maybe it's because he's got three sisters, but he talks to girls just like they're regular people. Not like some guys, who show off or act all dumb.

Of course, *those* guys act all nervous around a girl when they like her, which sends definite signals about their feelings. Not Brian. He always acts the same. He's always . . . Brian.

Which made it all the harder for me to figure out what he was thinking.

I crossed the street, jamming my hands into my jeans pockets.

Why hasn't Brian asked me out? I wondered.

That was the thing I needed to figure out. I mean, we were really good friends and we had kissed a couple of times, so I knew he *liked* me. But did he like me the way I wanted him to like me? The "I'm crazy about you and you're the most amazing girl in all of Sweet Valley" kind of way?

Because that's how I liked him.

Here's the whole story. Brian and I had kissed a couple of times, but we were far from a couple. I mean, we'd never really *discussed* the kissing thing, and we'd never gone out on an official date. We just sort of hung out a lot, and sometimes we wound up kissing.

I didn't mind the way things were, but I'd love to be able to say, "My boyfriend, Brian."

Then again . . . as long as Brian and I were *just friends,* we could be friends for a long time. Forever, even. But if we went out, we might break up. Then we might not be friends anymore.

7

The other possibility, which I couldn't even bear to really think about because it was so horrible, was that Brian was just using me. I mean, we really did hang out a lot, and since I was a girl and I was *there* . . . Maybe he just kissed me for something to do, but he didn't really like me in that way. And he didn't want to be my boyfriend.

In that case, I didn't want to be his friend.

I let out a long, miserable sigh. This whole thing was so complicated! I had no idea what to do.

But I'll know the truth soon enough, I reminded myself. The perfect opportunity was about to happen—the big Homecoming dance.

Homecoming is *the* social event at school. *All* the students are there, and even some kids from the high school come back to see the game and have a good time at the dance. It's absolutely huge.

Either Brian would ask me to the dance with him, or he'd ask someone else. That would pretty much tell me what I needed to know.

The only other way this whole thing could go was that *I* could ask *Brian* to the dance.

But what if he said no? I'd feel like a complete jerk. But at least I'd know that he *had* just been using me.

Or what if he said yes, but only because he

was too *nice* to say no? That would be just like Brian. And that wasn't the kind of yes I wanted.

Frustrated, I pushed open the door to my apartment building and crossed the lobby to the stairs. I took the stairs two at a time, feeling pretty stupid for getting all worked up over a silly dance.

But to tell the truth, I didn't know *what* to do.

And it was driving me completely nuts!

Wednesday Morning
Before First Period

7:30 A.M. Jessica stares down at the pile of blue glitter on the floor by her desk. She realizes that it must be coming off one of the posters leaning against her chair. Jessica worries that all the glitter will come off before she has a chance to hang them and pays no attention to her homeroom teacher, Mr. Edwards, who is reading announcements.

7:32 A.M. Ms. Fenton, sixth-grade science teacher, relaxes in the faculty lounge before her first-period class. She opens a science magazine and begins to read an article titled "Taking a Stand for Ecology."

7:38 A.M. Jessica has to sneak a peek at the posters to see if they're okay. She swivels in her seat. Mr. Edwards asks what she's doing.

7:39 A.M. Ms. Fenton finishes first page of article. Wonders if she's done enough to protect the environment. Vows to get tougher about environmental issues.

7:40 A.M. Jessica is relieved Mr. Edwards lightened up when she showed him her posters.

They're for a good cause, after all. Plus most of the glitter is still holding.

7:41 A.M.   Ms. Fenton decides to photocopy the article for her classes when she's finished reading it.

7:42 A.M.   Jessica tells Mr. Edwards she would like to hang some of the posters right before first period from 7:50 to 8:00. The posters get an enthusiastic response from the class, especially the one with the glittery dolphins captured in a net. Some wildcats on a boat are throwing the net. A line across the top reads Kill the Dolphins! The whole class cheers. *Yes!* Jessica thinks. People are noticing her! Mr. Edwards excuses Jessica from homeroom early to begin hanging her posters.

7:50 A.M.   Jessica begins to hang up her posters in the hallway, still beaming from all her classmates' attention.

7:53 A.M.   Ms. Fenton heads for the faculty copy room.

7:54 A.M.   Jessica makes a loop of masking tape and then attaches it to the back of a poster—the one with the net over the dolphins. Her best one.

7:55 A.M.   Ms. Fenton turns down hallway. Sees a girl taping a poster to the wall. Wonders if girl has pass to be out of class at this time.

7:57 A.M.   Jessica sees teacher approaching. Smiles at teacher and pretends to smooth poster as she waits for teacher to notice and compliment it.

7:59 A.M.   Ms. Fenton stops and stares at poster. "Did you do this?" she asks the girl.

7:59 A.M.   Jessica nods sheepishly. Then realizes there is a problem. This teacher looks angry. Very angry! Jessica steps back as teacher shouts something about advocating the massacre of dolphins.

8:00 A.M.   Homeroom period ends. Doors burst open. Hall fills with kids who stare as Ms. Fenton steers Jessica toward the principal's office. Jessica is mortified. This is not the kind of attention she wanted—not at all!

Damon

Like things weren't already bad enough.

Jessica had to walk in and see me sitting in the principal's office.

She aimed those amazing blue-green eyes right at me, and I wanted to melt into the floor.

I wanted to say something to her, but what?

Hi, it's me, Damon Ross, the guy who is hoping you like him. Yup, I'm just hanging out here like a loser waiting for the principal to give me his sermon. Want to hook up later?

Call me crazy, but I don't think so.

"Hey, Jessica," I mumbled instead.

She shot me a quick, tight smile, then rolled her eyes. That's when I noticed that Fish-face Fenton had walked in with her. One hand was clutched in a death grip on Jessica's arm, the other was waving a big piece of poster board around.

I wanted to yell, "Hey, Fenton! Get your fish hands off her!" But I wasn't exactly in a position

13

to do that. (And fish don't have hands anyway.)

I'd been called down to the principal's office to explain my "multiple latenesses and absences."

I didn't really know what to say about them. My mom works at night, and sometimes she's so tired, I have to let her sleep and watch my little sisters. Sometimes we get a sitter, but we can't really afford one full-time. And there's no way I could ever leave my sisters by themselves—they're way too young for that. Besides, I love hanging out with them. They're awesome.

If I happen to miss the bus in the morning, I can't exactly walk to school. The trailer park where we live is way across town. And there's no one around to drive me.

This past month I'd racked up "multiple latenesses and absences." But so what? It happens. If I have to watch my sisters and miss a little school, that's just the way it is—no big deal.

I glanced at the clock on the wall. Whoa! First period started in only about seven more minutes. If Principal Todd didn't come out of his office to yell at me soon, I'd have one more lateness to add to my legendary record.

At that moment Mr. Todd appeared. He steered his big belly my way. "Mr. Ross—"

"Mr. Todd," Ms. Fenton cut him off. "If you

don't mind, I'm due in class very soon, and I need to talk to you."

Todd turned away from me. "Certainly, Ms. Fenton, what is it?" he asked.

"I discovered this student, Ms. Wonkfeld—"

"*Wake*field," Jessica cut her off.

I smirked. *Wonkfeld?* How funny was that?

"Ms. Wakefield," Fenton said, "putting *this* on the wall!" She shoved the piece of poster board at him.

I sneaked a glance at the poster. It was a cute picture of some cats on a boat throwing sparkly nets onto a bunch of dolphins.

So? What's the problem with that? I wondered.

Todd stared at her, looking sort of dumb, like he didn't get it either.

The secretary, Ms. Hayes, leaned around her computer to have a look. She seemed clueless too.

"Kill the dolphins!" Fenton said angrily. "It says it right here." She ran her fingers back and forth across the writing, showering sparkles all over the carpet. "It's an outrage!"

Mr. Todd rubbed his hand across the little bit of hair left on the top of his head. "Ahh, I see," he mumbled, although I don't think he really did.

"It's just a team-spirit poster," Jessica spoke up. "You know, we're playing the Redwood *Dolphins* at the Homecoming game."

Fenton's face began to burn with embarrassment. Pink blotches broke out all over her cheeks. Obviously the Homecoming connection was total news to her.

"It doesn't matter," she insisted shrilly. "Team spirit doesn't have to be presented in a manner that condones the senseless slaughter of another species."

"True," Mr. Todd said, nodding. "Yes, that's true."

"But I wasn't thinking of it that way. Not at all," Jessica insisted, her forehead wrinkled in the cutest frown I've ever seen. "Honestly, that never occurred to me. I was only thinking about the teams."

That's one thing (of many) I like about Jessica. This wasn't the first time I'd seen her stand up for herself or for someone else. She's so amazingly brave.

"Ms. Wakefield, I have to agree with Ms. Fenton," Todd told her. "This sort of thing flies in the face of the very values we try to engender in Sweet Valley students."

Oh, man, I thought, and shook my head. Todd was on a roll, and he was really working the principal lingo.

My family moves around a lot, so I've been at a few schools in my life. Believe me, *all* principals talk like that. I mean, why couldn't he just say, "We don't want our students thinking it's cool to kill dolphins"?

Mr. Todd continued. "I have no choice here but to assign you a week of after-school detention, Ms. Wakefield."

"Oh, please don't," Jessica pleaded. She looked really upset. "I didn't mean to do anything wrong! And besides, it's not like anyone will actually go out and *kill* dolphins because of my poster. Look, they're only *netting* the dolphins. Maybe they just want to take them to Sea World or something."

"It says 'Kill the Dolphins' right on the poster!" Fenton screeched.

"I know," Jessica admitted. "But I could change it to something else. How about . . . um . . . *Stop the Dolphins?*" She looked up at Mr. Todd. "Would that be better?"

Todd glanced at Fenton, whose face was all pinched up like she was seriously annoyed.

I had to cough to keep myself from laughing out loud. Now she looked even more like a fish than before!

"It just occurred to me," Todd announced, stroking his chin thoughtfully. "I don't think you should use the poster at all since the picture is still in questionable taste. But to prove you really have school spirit, I'm going to give you an assignment rather than detention."

Jessica narrowed her eyes suspiciously. "What kind of assignment?" she asked.

"Well, the ninth-grade student who was formerly in charge of the Homecoming dance just informed me that her family is moving away and that she won't be able to continue her duties. So, instead of detention, you're going to take over as head of the dance committee."

I had to hand it to Principal Todd—he wasn't as mean as I thought. Asking a girl like Jessica to plan a dance is like giving her a huge present. It's certainly not punishment.

Jessica's face totally lit up. "Sure! I mean, absolutely! Wow! You have *so* picked the right person for this. I throw the best parties! You won't be sorry!"

"I have to get to my class," Fenton said, her voice all huffy. She turned and left the room.

"Thank you, Mr. Todd," Jessica said. She was so excited, she even grabbed his hand and shook it. I almost burst out laughing again when I saw his stunned expression.

Every time I see Jessica, she gets more and more amazing. Maybe someday soon I'd be able to tell her that.

"You'd better get to class," Todd said.

As Jessica turned to leave, she smiled at me. "See you later, Damon," she said. Then she mouthed, "Good luck," jerking her head in Todd's direction.

"Thanks," I mouthed back, and watched her disappear out the door.

The way she'd said *good luck,* with such a mischievous grin, put a whole new spin on my situation. All of a sudden I really didn't mind that I was about to have my own face-to-face with Mr. Todd. After Jessica's stellar performance, I figured I'd try to stick up for myself and talk to Todd in his own language rather than apologize pathetically like I always did.

"Now, Mr. Ross." Todd turned toward me.

"Mr. Todd," I said. "I would like to point out that right now I'm late for my first class. But that's okay with me. I mean, it just shows you how latenesses can happen in a series of circumstances over which no one has control."

It worked! You should have seen Todd's face. Total shock.

"Uh . . . well . . . yes," he said, totally caught off guard. "You'd better get to class. We'll discuss this at a more convenient time."

I smiled and made my way toward history class.

No wonder I like Jessica so much—she's inspiring.

Elizabeth

"No! No way! You can't write that!" I gasped. "But write it anyway!" Then I started laughing so hard, I slipped off the inflatable chair in my room.

That set the whole *Zone* staff off into another laughing frenzy. Tears streamed down Anna Wang's face. Brian Rainey was doubled over, clutching his stomach. And Salvador del Valle was practically barking, he was laughing so hard.

"Okay, okay. Come on, guys, we've got to settle down," I said as I crawled back into my chair.

"*Hiccup!*" I let out the loudest hiccup I'd ever heard. I had to get control of myself.

I knew we were being silly, but that happens a lot when we're working on *Zone*, the 'zine we started as an alternative to the school newspaper.

We were putting together the second issue on the computer in my bedroom. We write lots of funny, spoofy things in *Zone*. Which is why we get so out of control sometimes.

"Hiccup!"

"Ms. Wakefield." Salvador giggled. "Please! We're working here."

"Stand on your head," Brian suggested.

Anna wiped her face on her sleeve, her shoulders still shaking.

"What?" I demanded, confused.

"My sister Ellie gets hiccups all the time. She gets rid of them by doing a headstand," Brian explained.

Considering the fact that I was wearing a very short T-shirt that would be impossible to tuck into my jeans before I turned upside down, I decided to take less drastic measures and headed to the bathroom for a cup of water.

When I returned, everyone was back to business, reading Brian's story on my computer. It was about an alien landing in the middle of the Homecoming events. The funny part was, it was written from the alien's point of view.

> *I spied their leader at once. She stood on a large platform covered with flowering plant life. A sign below her read Homecoming Queen. (The queen was clearly noteworthy for being markedly cuter than the other life-forms.)*
>
> *I searched the blue skies, looking for those life-forms who would be returning home, but I*

saw none. How odd. If no one was coming home, why was this called Homecoming?

On the ground, helmeted, big-shouldered beings scurried by. Their numbered chests told me they were lower life-forms, probably brainless clones, numbered in order to tell them apart.

The *brainless clones* part was what set us all off.

Salvador turned to Brian. "You sure you want to get the football team mad? Because if they come after you, I'm not backing you up, man," he joked.

Brian waved him off. "I know all those guys. When they see I wrote it, they'll understand it's a joke. They know I don't have anything against jocks."

"Why don't you add a part where they save the alien from the Redwood team?" Anna suggested. "That might soften it."

"It could be funny too," Brian agreed. He started to laugh again. "And like maybe some girl asks the alien to the dance—"

"Meet the new chair of the Homecoming dance committee!"

We all whirled around. My twin, Jessica, stood in my doorway, practically glowing with excitement.

"Chairperson of the Homecoming dance? How did that happen?" I asked. I had to admit this was Jessica's dream come true. She loves planning parties—in fact, she'd planned a huge one at the beginning of school. In our house. And we'd both gotten in major trouble for it. At least this party would be legal.

Jessica came in and sat down on the end of my bed. Then she told us the unbelievable story about getting into trouble for her Kill the Dolphins poster. Only Jessica could start out with detention and end up as head of the dance committee. Talk about luck.

"I had Fish-face Fenton for science," Brian said. "She's got zero sense of humor."

"I know. But this totally great thing came out of it!" Jessica smiled. "Liz, you'll be on my committee, won't you?" she asked me.

"Sorry, Jess. I just don't think I can fit it in," I said. "This issue is way behind schedule already."

I felt a small pang of guilt. The truth was that if I'd been dying to do it, I probably *could* have scheduled it in. But the idea of working on a dance committee just didn't thrill me. Anyway, if I thought Jessica wouldn't be able to get help, I'd be in. But she had other friends like Bethel and Kristin and Damon. I was sure they would be only too happy to help.

"*Elizabeth,*" Jessica pleaded.

"*Jessica,*" I pleaded back, imitating her.

"Fine," she huffed. She shifted her attention to Brian. "At least I can count on *you*, right, Brian?"

Brian shifted uneasily in his chair. "Ummm . . . I don't know."

"*Kristin* will be on the committee . . . ," she almost sang out instead of speaking in a normal voice.

A shot of pink tinged Brian's cheeks, but it disappeared in a snap. If Jessica had embarrassed him, he fought it well. "I'll think about it, okay?" Brian told her. "We can talk later."

"No problem." Jessica got up from the bed. "I'd better get on the phone. I'm getting *everyone* to help. I can't wait—this is going to be the coolest Homecoming dance ever."

"Wow, she was really dying to have *us* on her committee," Anna remarked to Salvador when Jessica had left.

Ouch. I'd hoped they wouldn't notice that she hadn't asked them. It's no secret that Jessica doesn't have much use for any of my friends, except Brian.

To Jessica, Brian is cool because he's part of Kristin's group. Besides the fact that he's really a nice person—and that he's friends with practically everyone in school.

"Yeah," Salvador said. He leaned back and

placed his hands behind his head. "She probably knew we were way too cool and in demand to be on her committee."

Anna laughed.

Good, I thought. They didn't seem freaked out about it.

Salvador leaned forward in his chair. "Her Dolphins story gave me an idea, though. Why don't we write something about it and then add other headlines that would upset Fenton? Like 'Yankees Destroy Baltimore Orioles' or 'Mariners Stomp Toronto Blue Jays.'"

"Oooh! Wait! I have one . . . ," Anna said.

We were at it again. I smiled at my group of friends. Jessica might not like them, but they meant a lot to me. . . .

If only Jessica had a group of friends like this, she'd be so much happier.

I hoped she was right—that this would be the best Homecoming dance ever. If Jessica could really pull this off and make it good, she might actually stop worrying so much about fitting in at our new school. She'd had such a hard time ever since we started at SVJH. This might just give her the boost she needed.

Damon

I snuck around the bookstore, making sure to glance left and right every few feet.

I knew exactly where I was headed—I just had to make sure no one saw me.

Wait a second. Relax, I thought. *It's not like you're shoplifting or anything. You're just buying a magazine.*

Trouble was, it wasn't just *any* magazine I wanted. It was *TeenTalk*. Yeah, that's right, *TeenTalk*—that fashion magazine for girls.

Trust me, it's not like I wanted it for the makeup samples or anything. It's just that when I was in the same bookstore last week, checking out the latest issue of *Xtreme*, one of the *TeenTalk* headlines kind of jumped out at me. It said, "Homecoming Heaven: Girls Give the Scoop on Dream-Date Essentials!"

An article full of girls talking about what makes an excellent Homecoming date! It was perfect! Just what I needed so I wouldn't majorly blow things with Jessica.

Not that I'd actually asked her to Homecoming or anything yet. But I was going to. Especially after that great smile she gave me in the principal's office this morning.

But first I wanted to get the info on how to do things right.

Last week Mom was in the bookstore with me, so I couldn't buy the magazine. That's why I went back for it.

See, dances aren't really my natural habitat. I'm happier hanging out at home or at Vito's Pizza. Or out on the lacrosse field.

First of all, I don't dance. I mean, I've never really tried.

Second, these Homecoming things are a lot fancier than regular school dances. My usual jeans and flannel shirt won't cut it. I'm on a tight budget, but hopefully Mom would help me spring for something nice for a special occasion.

Third, I wanted Jessica to have the time of her life at the dance. I just wasn't sure how to make that happen.

I needed help.

I spotted the magazine. (Which was pretty easy. The whole front of it was covered in bright pink writing.) It was time to make my move.

I glanced at the checkout counter. No one I knew was working there. So what if the guy thought I was strange? I'd never see him again. Hopefully.

Walking quickly to the shelf, I snapped up the magazine and hurried to the cashier. I was almost there when some guy stepped in between me and the counter.

Argh! That meant I had to stand on line, waiting, with the stupid magazine in my hand.

I rolled it up and shifted anxiously from foot to foot.

"Hey, Damon."

I whipped around and saw Brian Rainey standing behind me, with a book in his hands.

I clutched the magazine even tighter. *Act cool,* I coached myself. *Maybe he won't notice what you're buying.*

"Hey." I nodded at Brian.

"What'd you get?" Brian asked, pointing at the magazine under my arm.

Oh, man! Busted! I thought. I glanced down at the magazine. The neon orange-and-pink lip-gloss ad on the back of it was clearly visible.

"Uh, just a magazine. You know, for my sisters," I answered. *Right.* My sisters couldn't even read!

"*TeenTalk?*" Brian asked. Did he have x-ray vision? "Right on."

"Uh, well," I muttered, feeling the color rising to my cheeks. "I—"

"Yeah," Brian interrupted. "Ellie, my older sister, has a subscription to that. I steal it from her all the time. It's pretty funny."

"Really?" I gulped, taken aback.

"Yeah. Anyway, I'm going to go check out some skiing magazines. See you later," Brian said. Then he moved on toward the sports section.

"See ya," I said casually, and breathed out in relief.

I gave the cashier my money, rolled the magazine up tight once more, and headed for the door.

I couldn't tell whether Brian thought I was a total loser or not, but I sure felt like one.

Still, it would all be worth it if I got some clue about what to do with Jessica at the dance.

The magazine had better be good.

Jessica's Recruiting Campaign
Wednesday

11:55 A.M. Lunch. Jessica tells Kristin all about what happened that morning and how she's heading the Homecoming dance committee. They clink milk cartons in celebration. Jessica asks if she can count on Kristin to help. Kristin panics. She's already really, really busy since she's head of the poster committee on top of being class president. Jessica mentions that *Brian* is on her committee. Kristin promises to find a way to squeeze it into her schedule.

2:10 P.M. Before track practice Jessica asks her track pal Bethel McCoy to join her committee. Bethel snorts. She's not going to plan a dance she doesn't even want to go to. Jessica looks so disappointed that Bethel relents. She tells Jessica she's been looking for something school oriented to do since she lost the election for class president anyway. She agrees to be on the committee.

3:45 P.M. After track practice Jessica heads back

to the locker room. Jessica spots Brian in the hall and asks if he's made up his mind about the committee. He doesn't seem too sure. Jessica says Kristin will be *so* disappointed if he decides not to join. Brian hastily agrees to be on the committee.

3:50 P.M. Jessica goes back to her locker to get her books to take home, fretting about asking Damon to be on the committee. Will he still like her if she has to act like his boss? If she doesn't ask him to be on the committee, won't he feel left out? Just then her locker partner, Ronald Rheece, shows up. He mentions that he's heard Jessica is in need of volunteers for her committee. Jessica cringes. This can't be happening. Ronald squares his puny shoulders and beams up at her. It *is* happening. Ronald volunteers for the committee.

3:53 P.M. Jessica calls Damon from the pay phone at school to ask if he'd mind helping her out with the dance, stressing the fact that the two of them will have to work *very* closely together. Damon agrees, wondering worriedly how he'll ever get enough time away from watching his sisters.

3:56 P.M.   Jessica heads home, glowing happily. Her committee rules. (Well, except for Ronald.) All her new friends will be together in one place. Maybe this could be their chance to really bond, and she'll be part of a group again like she was at her old school. Without doubt, this is going to be the best Homecoming dance Sweet Valley Junior High has ever seen!

Jessica

Thursday after last period, I headed for the empty classroom—room 206—where I had arranged to hold my first dance-committee meeting. My stomach was full of butterflies. I'd been looking forward to this all day.

"Good luck, Jess," Elizabeth called from down the hall, and held up two crossed fingers. I waved back at her and walked inside.

Brian was already there, drawing cute little martians on the blackboard in yellow chalk.

"Hey, Jessica," he said. "Like my drawings?"

Actually, they weren't all that bad. "Save your creativity," I said, laughing. "We need to make lots of decorations for the dance."

Brian grabbed a chair and sat in it sideways, drumming on the desk. I rummaged through my book bag, pulling out a notebook and pencil to make lists of what we'd need for the dance. I leaned against the teacher's desk and wrote down the name of each person on the committee. The first thing I wanted to do was assign tasks.

Jessica

Just then Kristin appeared in the doorway. She spotted Brian and made a beeline for the seat next to his.

"Hey, guys," she said, smiling. "Nice martians. Did you draw those, Jess?"

"No way!" I protested, laughing.

"Hey," Brian said, raising his eyebrows at Kristin. "You think you could do better?"

Instead of one of her usual quick comebacks, Kristin looked down at her feet and blushed. *What's up with that?* I wondered.

Just then Ronald and Bethel came in, followed by Damon.

Ronald pulled up a chair so that he was sitting really close to where I was standing.

Bethel sat a few rows back from Brian and Kristin. And Damon sat in the corner. Not exactly what you'd call a unified group. But they would be by Homecoming. I'd make sure of it.

"Hello, everyone," Ronald said brightly, looking straight up at me.

No one responded.

"Hey, guys," I said. I backed away from Ronald and hoisted myself up on the teacher's desk. "Thanks for coming. This dance is going to be the best ever, and I know you guys have a lot of ideas. So let's get to work."

So far, so good, I thought. It was a semi-inspiring

pep talk—not too formal and not too bossy.

"The first thing we need to decide is who's in charge of what," I told the group, "so I'm going to assign jobs to—"

"Shouldn't we settle on a theme before we do anything else?" Bethel jumped in.

I paused, frowning. I hadn't really thought about a theme yet. "Well, maybe—"

"Themes are dorky," Kristin cut her off. "Let's work the whole dance around some colors instead. My cousin Lisa's school in New York has a dance every year called The Silver and Gold. Doesn't that sound totally sophisticated? Since this is Homecoming, I say we use the school colors, silver and blue."

Bethel glared at her. "Every Homecoming in the history of Sweet Valley Junior High has had a theme," she argued. "Besides, silver and blue are boring colors."

"I agree. Totally boring," Brian put in.

"But—" Kristin stared at Brian. Even I was surprised that he'd backed Bethel up instead of her.

Uh-oh, I thought. *Trouble in paradise.*

"How about purple and yellow?" Bethel said. "Now, that could be cool."

"Yeah! Definitely way better than silver and blue," Brian agreed.

Kristin shook her head and glared at Brian. She looked really angry.

"Excuse me, but purple and yellow might be an invitation for trouble," Ronald stated seriously.

"What do you mean, trouble?" Bethel challenged.

"Scientific evidence suggests that overly vivid colors in a crowd setting can excite emotions and encourage violent physical activity," he explained.

"Whoa," Damon put in from his seat in the corner. "You mean kids might start dancing too fast or something?"

I giggled, but no one else seemed to find it amusing. *What's wrong with everyone?* I wondered. *This is supposed to be fun!*

"That's one possible effect, but I'm worried that bright colors might also incite arguments, even fighting," Ronald insisted.

"Oh, please." Bethel laughed.

"Guys—listen," I cut in. "We've kind of gotten off track here. I'd like to stick to my original plan and make assignments first."

"You're the boss," Damon said.

I stopped. I could feel my face turning hot and red. *Boss?* But I didn't want to be the boss. I just wanted to plan a fun dance! Was I being too bossy? Whatever—I had to keep going.

"Um—I just want to stick to my plan," I said

hastily, picking up my notebook. "Now, I'd like to read you a list of assignments I made."

"Go ahead," Brian encouraged.

"Okay," I began. "Damon, I've assigned you to lifting, carrying, and moving all the heavy stuff while we're setting up. Brian, I thought you'd be good on decorating and—"

"Wait a second—how come I'm doing all the lifting?" Damon objected.

"Yeah. What's up with that?" Brian sputtered. He shot a sideways glance at Kristin. "I can carry stuff too, you know. I'm not a total wimp."

"Yeah. Let him carry stuff," Damon agreed. "And I can decorate."

"Wait, wait, wait," Brian interrupted. "I didn't say I didn't want to decorate. I just said I could lift stuff too."

Kristin stood up and held out her arms like a referee. "Look, let's not fight," she said.

"Sit down, Kristin," Bethel grumbled from behind her. "Being class president doesn't mean you're in charge of everything."

"I was just trying to help." Kristin turned and snapped at her. "And besides, I've been on lots of committees. I know how things like this get done."

What's happening? I wondered, getting anxious when I saw my friends' tense, angry expressions. *Why are they being like this?*

37

Ronald got to his feet. Kristin didn't look like she was finished talking, but that didn't stop him from launching into a speech. "Let's be clear-headed about this," he began. "There's no need to quarrel. We need an organizational focus. Perhaps we should draft a statement setting out our mission in this committee and then . . ."

He kept blabbing on about a mission statement, but nobody was listening.

I stared at my friends. They seemed to have forgotten that the reason we were meeting was to plan the Homecoming dance. And that they were there to help *me*. They weren't even looking at me anymore! They were too busy glaring and pouting at each other. I had to do something—fast!

I climbed up and stood on top of the teacher's desk

"Quiet! Please!" I shouted over Ronald's jabbering.

He stopped, and everyone looked up at me, their eyes wide.

"Thank you," I said. I blew a strand of blond hair away from my face, stalling for time. I hadn't really thought about what I was going to say. I just wanted them to stop bickering.

Ronald hurried up to me. "Jessica, let me help you down from there." He held out his arms. "Jump and I'll catch you."

I glared down at him. "Ronald, I can get

down myself," I growled. I stepped down onto the teacher's chair and jumped to the floor.

Ronald was at my side, his clammy hand fluttering up to my elbow. "You might have really hurt yourself," he insisted.

"I think she can take care of herself, Ronald," Damon grumbled from the corner. I flashed him a thankful smile.

Damon glanced at his watch. "Jessica—I'm really sorry, but I think I'd better go." He stood up and shoved his hands in his pockets, shrugging apologetically.

I felt myself panic. If Damon left now, he might never come back! Why was he leaving? I had to get rid of Ronald! I lunged forward to grab Damon's arm. "Wait! Wait just one second—okay?" Then I turned back to Ronald.

"I need you do something very important," I told him. Ronald stared back at me with his muddy brown eyes, nodding seriously. "Go and figure out the square footage of the gym. I know no one else will be able to do that as well as you."

I glanced behind me to see if Damon was sitting back down again. But he had already picked up his backpack and was heading for the door. "See you all later," he called. I stared after him. Oh no! Did Damon think I was ignoring him when I was talking to Ronald? That had so not been the plan. Didn't he see I was trying to *get rid* of Ronald?

Ronald pulled his calculator from his pocket, oblivious to Damon's exit. "Would you like the measurements in metric units or standard?" he asked me.

"Whatever," I said miserably. "Centimeters are good."

Ronald hurried out to measure the gym. At least I had one overeager dance planner. No one else seemed into it at all. It's not like I'd asked them to build a pyramid or anything either.

I whirled around, still clutching my notepad.

Kristin, Brian, and Bethel were staring back at me, their arms folded, their faces sour and threatening. They looked more like a firing squad than the group of fun, cool, sweet friends I'd always wanted.

"Look," I said, flustered. "Why don't we all think about what we want this dance to be like? We can meet again tomorrow at my house and really get going with our plans. I . . . I really appreciate all your help."

Bethel and Brian smiled. No, smirked—they were smirking! At me! My so-called friends!

Bethel jumped up and headed for the door. "Later," she called, and I actually felt glad to see her go.

I turned and fumbled for my backpack, feeling kind of shaky.

Behind me I could hear Brian and Kristin leaving. Separately. What was their deal anyway?

Desperately, I looked around the empty classroom. What was I going to do? The dance was going to be a flop at this rate.

Maybe the next meeting will go better, I reassured myself. *It's not like things could get any worse.*

Thursday Night
Instant Messages between
Brian and Kristin

KGrl99: Hey, Brian. How's it going? :)

BRainE: Okay, now that my 8 tons of math homework are done. That meeting was fun, huh?

KGrl99: lol. Tell me about it. And since you mentioned it, blue and silver are *not* boring. Where's your school spirit?

BRainE: Don't yell. I just thought it would be fun to do something different, that's all.

KGrl99: Maybe.

BRainE: Definitely.

KGrl99: But Bethel is totally bossy, don't you think?

BRainE: No comment.

KGrl99: What's that supposed to mean?

BRainE: It *means,* no comment.

KGrl99: Fine.

BRainE: Fine.

KGrl99: Look, I gotta go.

BRainE: Wait!

BRainE: Kristin?

Damon

Man, I hated having to run out of Jessica's meeting like that. But when I checked my watch, I knew I had to move. My mom had a doctor's appointment and had left my sisters with a baby-sitter in Briggs Heights, the neighborhood where we live. I had to be at the sitter's place at four to pick up my sisters and walk them home.

As soon as Mom got home, I had about an hour to myself before she left for work. An hour to research my transformation into Jessica's perfect Homecoming date.

I ripped the *TeenTalk* article out of the magazine, shoved it in my pocket, and hopped on a bus to the mall. On the bus I took the article out of my pocket and read over the first few paragraphs.

> *"I love it when my date shows up wearing a totally killer outfit," says Sarah, a high-school sophomore. "It shows he took the time*

to make himself look good for me and that he really cares about our date."

Okay, one thing was clear—I had to make myself look good.

When I got to the mall, I headed into a men's store that looked pretty busy. I took a quick look at the racks. Pants, shirts, sweaters, jackets—all in a ton of different colors and materials. Some looked really shiny and trendy, and some looked like something my history teacher would wear. Now I knew why I stuck to jeans.

What is Jessica's favorite color? I wondered.

I picked up a pair of pants in greenish blue made out of this really high-tech iridescent material. Hmmm. They were totally not my thing, but I liked blue, and they were kind of the same color as Jessica's eyes. *Maybe they'd look cool with that bright yellow shirt on the rack over there,* I thought. I picked up the pants and headed over to the shirt.

"Uh—excuse me—you weren't going to wear those *together,* were you?"

I turned and saw a redheaded woman staring at me with a worried expression on her face. Her name tag said Sonya.

I smiled, a little embarrassed. Make that a lot embarrassed. "Hi. I need to buy something to wear to my Homecoming dance. Something that will look good—"

"A Homecoming dance? How *cute!*" Sonya interrupted in a kind of loud voice. I glanced around, hoping no one had heard her.

"Come with me—I know just what you need!" Sonya grabbed my arm. I followed her around the store while she piled stuff into my arms. Then she led me into the dressing room and waited outside for me to model my new outfit.

Eventually I got everything on and stepped out of the room. I checked myself out in the store's big mirror.

Whoa! I had to admit, I looked—well, *good!* I had on a pair of black pants with a little stretch to them, a really soft gray T-shirt, black shoes (*real* shoes, not work boots or sneakers), a black belt with a cool silver buckle, and a black jacket with four buttons down the front.

"Do you like it?" Sonya asked.

"Yeah!" I told her. "How much is—" I glanced at the price tag on the sleeve of the jacket. No way!

I lunged back in the dressing room and ripped everything off. I could feel myself getting hot—I just wanted to get out of there. I grabbed the soft gray T-shirt and brought it out with me.

"I'll take this, please," I told Sonya. "Just this."

Jessica

Dear Diary,

If this dance bombs, I'm toast.

No. I have to stop thinking all these negative thoughts. I'm going to organize an amazing homecoming. I have to.

I just have to make it more fun for my friends so they don't fight.

Kristin and Bethel? What was up with that? I mean, shouldn't they be over that whole running-for-class-president rivalry thing? The election was like weeks ago. Then Brian sides with Bethel instead of Kristin. Hello? Random! And Brian getting all defensive about me not asking him to do the heavy lifting! Duh—his arms are like twigs!

Who even knows what Damon was thinking? Not me.

Hopefully tomorrow will go better. The meeting is here at home, so everyone can just hang out and relax. I'll serve snacks and play music, kind of set the party mood.

And instead of assigning jobs, I'll let everyone decide what they want to do. Then everyone will be happy, no one will fight, and everything will be perfect.

Here's what we need to talk about:

1. Music. (A band's probably too expensive, so I want to find the best DJ!)
2. Lighting. (I vote for dark and romantic.)
3. Decorations. (Guess I'll just throw that one out there for the group.)
4. Posters and flyers. (Ditto.)
5. Chaperons. (Unfortunately we have to have them. Might as well make sure we get cool ones.)
6. Food!!!!

I can't think of anything else right now. If I forgot anything, I'm sure someone will remind me.

One thing I can't plan, but I hope it happens. It has to happen!

Damon has to ask me to the dance. Soon!

Jessica

Chips? Check. Soda? Check. Popcorn? *It's in the microwave.* I took a mental survey of everything I needed for my Friday meeting.

"Par-tay!" my big brother, Steven, shouted, bouncing obnoxiously up and down on the living-room couch. His eyes lit up at the sight of all the food. Mom says the only thing sixteen-year-old boys think about besides girls is food. Steven looked ready to pounce.

"Stay back," I warned, spreading my hands over my snacks. "They're for my meeting."

Out front a horn honked. It had to be for Steven since none of my friends drive. Inside the kitchen the microwave beeped. Steven looked torn for a second, like he was weighing the benefits. Friends or popcorn? He got up and bounded toward the front door. "Save me some," he shouted as he walked out to meet his friends.

Don't count on it, I thought as I went into the kitchen to grab the nuked popcorn. I poured it into a big plastic bowl and set it on the coffee table. Then I popped in a CD.

The doorbell rang. It was Brian. "Hey," he said when I opened the door. I led him into the living room, and he plopped himself down on the couch, practically diving into the warm popcorn in front of him. The doorbell rang again.

In the next few minutes the whole group arrived.

"This is great, isn't it? Help yourself to anything you want," I said happily as I perched on the arm of our couch. "So, let's get started. I've made a list of topics to cover—"

"I'm sorry, everyone, but I just can't picture the dance looking right in purple and yellow," Kristin cut in. "I've really been thinking about it, and it just doesn't work for me."

"If you don't like purple and yellow, pick something else." Bethel shrugged.

I smiled at Bethel. It was nice of her to be so reasonable.

"Fine. I pick blue and silver," Kristin said, crossing her arms over her chest.

"Anything *except* blue and silver," Bethel said through clenched teeth.

Uh-oh! Tension alert. I had to do something to diffuse the situation. I stepped between Kristin and Bethel. "Popcorn?" I offered, holding out the bowl.

Jessica

"I'll have some," Ronald said from the far end of the couch. He took the entire bowl of popcorn and planted it on his lap. "Jessica, I made some notes on the dance last night," he said, his mouth full of popcorn.

At least someone is putting some effort into this, I thought. *Even if it is Ronald.* He reached into his school backpack. "Here they are," he said, and handed me a wad of papers almost an inch thick.

I took the notes and glanced over at Kristin and Bethel, who were scowling angrily at each other.

I need to get over there. Fast, I thought, starting to panic.

"I was inspired by my measurements of the gym," Ronald began explaining. "I noticed its square footage was equally divisible by seven. This seemed to present amazing potential for space management. I made some calculations right here to demonstrate how the space might be broken up into sevenths."

"Ronald—" I tried to stop him, but he kept going—showing me his calculations. Not only was he boring me to death, but Bethel looked like she was on the verge of body slamming Kristin onto the carpet.

The tension-o-meter was way in the red zone.

I had to do something before things got ugly!

"Ronald—stop. Just for a second," I insisted, and turned away from him.

But I was a moment too late.

"You know what your problem is, Bethel?" Kristin shouted, bolting up from her seat.

Bethel jumped up to face her. "What?"

"You think you know everything!"

"Me?"

I had to save this meeting—*now!*

But before I could say anything, Brian spoke up.

"Hey, come on, Kristin," he said. "Lighten up. Everyone can be a little on the bossy side sometimes."

Bethel smirked at Kristin. "Gee, Brian," she asked. "Talking about anyone I know?"

Uh-oh, I thought. Kristin's eyes were growing shiny with tears. She glanced back and forth from Bethel to Brian.

Damon leaned forward on the couch. "Um, guys, we have—" He paused. "Hey! Ronald, do me a favor and stop chewing so loudly? This is serious."

Kristin spoke over Damon, ignoring him. Her voice had become tight and high-pitched. "I can't believe you just said that, Brian!" she cried. "I can't believe you just said I was bossy!"

"Kristin, wait. That's not what I said," Brian defended himself.

Jessica

I curled my fists into tight balls at my sides. I wanted to scream, *Do any of you realize how important this dance is to me? Would you just be quiet and get along?* But no one was even looking at me anymore. They were too busy arguing.

Elizabeth came down the stairs just then. Either she used her twin telepathy and "knew" I was in trouble, or she heard all the screaming from her room and wanted to see what was going on.

She took in all the unhappy faces, then locked eyes with me. I stared back at her helplessly.

"Anyone want more popcorn?" she offered in a voice loud enough to cut through all the arguing.

For a second the room was silent. "I do," Ronald called out.

"Maybe you should lay off the food for a while, Ronald," Damon countered, his blue eyes smoldering. "It's kind of rude to just sit there stuffing your face."

"I'm not!" Ronald whined.

Then it all started up again. Everyone began arguing at once.

I looked down at the beige carpet, trying to block out their voices. What could I do?

"Jessica?"

I looked up. It was Ronald. He had chunks of

yellow popcorn wedged between his teeth.

"I was thinking we could break the room into seven equal parts," he told me. "In one we could have a brass band playing. In the second maybe a dinosaur section would be interesting. Maybe we could even have a fossil dig."

At that moment something inside me snapped.

"Stop it!" I shrieked. "Stop it! Stop it!"

Everyone stopped talking and turned to stare at me.

"This meeting is totally out of control. I want all of you out of my house! This definitely isn't working. The next meeting will be in the cafeteria. Monday. After school. Got it?"

"Got it," Damon answered, standing up. He headed for the door, holding it open until everyone had filed out. Then he shut the door behind him.

I never thought I'd be happy to see them go, especially Damon. But I was. I really was. In fact, just the thought of seeing them on Monday was more than I could bear. Here I was, trying to plan a dance. A great party that they could all go to and have fun at, and all they could do was fight. They were such jerks!

Elizabeth walked out of the kitchen, holding a fresh bowl of hot popcorn. "Where did everyone go?" she demanded.

53

"I threw them out," I told her. "I couldn't take it any longer."

"But—Jessica! They're your committee!"

"Some committee!" I shouted.

"Was it worse than the first meeting?" Elizabeth asked incredulously. I'd told her all about the fiasco that had been yesterday's meeting. I didn't think things could get any worse. Clearly they could.

"Much worse." I flopped down on the sofa and cracked open a can of soda. Then I told her the whole horrible story.

"Now everyone seriously hates each other. What's the point of having friends if they can't all get along?" I moaned.

"They don't hate each other," Elizabeth reasoned. "They just have different opinions on things."

"Well, they must hate *me,* then. Why else would they be so horrible?" I left out the part about how *I* was starting to feel about *them.* Just the thought of their stubborn, glaring faces made me cringe.

"They don't hate you," Elizabeth insisted.

"Damon hates me."

"No, he doesn't."

"Oh, Liz, what am I going to do?" I asked her desperately.

But for once my levelheaded, voice-of-reason twin didn't have an answer.

Kristin

"Who are you, and why are you calling me this early?" Jessica mumbled as she picked up the line.

"It's me. Kristin," I said. It was eight-thirty on Saturday morning, and I hadn't been able to sleep. I couldn't do anything but think about the meeting at Jessica's house the night before. I felt really upset about it. I had to talk to Jessica.

"Can you believe it?" I asked.

"What?" Jessica yawned. "What time is it anyway?"

"I mean, Brian's supposed to be my friend!" I interrupted. "I thought he liked me. How could he side with Bethel like that?"

Jessica didn't say anything for a minute. Then she yawned again. Or maybe it was a sigh.

"Kristin," she said slowly, "he didn't exactly side with Bethel."

"Yes, he did!" I insisted. "He called me bossy right in front of everyone!"

Jessica didn't answer.

"I mean, I don't think I'm bossy. I'm not. Right?"

"No. I don't think you're bossy," Jessica said, sounding bored. "I think Brian was just trying to stop you guys from fighting, and you took it the wrong way."

"I don't know, Jess." A lump formed in my throat. "Maybe—maybe he likes *Bethel*."

"Oh, please," Jessica snapped. "Brian likes *you*, okay? He likes *you*. You're just too sensitive about him."

"You think?" I asked.

"I know," she insisted.

I felt a little better when she said that.

Sometimes I wished I didn't like Brian so, *so* much. It might make things easier.

"Anyway, Kristin," Jessica said. "You have to help me—this dance is a disaster!"

"What do you mean?" I asked.

"Well, just look at the way things are going!" she said. "I mean, Ronald wants to build dinoland in the middle of the gym," she informed me.

"Dinoland?" I asked.

"Oh, never mind," she said. "I'm just praying Monday's meeting will be better than the one yesterday."

"Okay," I said. "I'll see you then."

"Yeah," Jessica sort of mumbled. "See you then." Then she hung up.

I hung up and started to clean up my room. I didn't want to stray too far from the phone in case Brian called to say he was sorry about yesterday.

I looked at my watch. It was almost nine. I'd give him until noon. If he didn't call by then, I was going to have to take drastic measures and call him myself.

I stared at the phone, willing it to ring.

Nothing.

Elizabeth

"Please be on my committee, Liz," Jessica pleaded with me on Monday morning. "You've done this kind of stuff before. You're organized and serious, and I'm sure you can keep everyone from fighting."

Poor Jessica. She was driving herself nuts over this dance. I knew things must be really bad since she'd followed me all the way back to my locker to grovel, which is not exactly her style.

"Jessica!" I replied. "I told you, I can't. I just don't have the time."

She sighed and leaned up against the locker beside mine. "*Please?*" she whined. "I need at least one sane person."

"Look, you can do this! Really," I reassured her. "You just have to get everyone to agree about one thing and then take it from there."

"You make it sound easy," she complained.

"Maybe you should just skip the subject of decorations for now. Talk about the music or something. And try to keep Kristin and Bethel busy doing separate things."

"How?" she asked.

"I don't know," I answered truthfully. I wished I could be more helpful. But my mind was actually on our latest issue of *Zone*. We were running late on production, and the students' response to our first issue was so good, we wanted to make sure we got the next one out as soon as we could. Besides, these were Jessica's friends we were talking about, not mine. I was sure she could handle it. "Listen, Jess. I've got to go," I said, slamming my locker shut.

"Fine. Go on." Jessica hung her head. She looked pretty pathetic. "Leave me alone. I can deal."

I did feel bad for leaving her, even if she was being overly melodramatic. But Jessica is tough—and resourceful. I knew she'd figure something out soon enough.

"Sorry, Jess," I said. "I'll see you later."

On my way to Salvador's locker I saw one of my least-favorite people heading toward me. Charlie Roberts—the editor of the school paper, the *Spectator*.

There are a few choice words to describe Charlie. Conceited. Mean. Obnoxious. Rude. You get the idea.

Charlie is the main reason we started *Zone*.

Elizabeth

When school started this year, Anna, Salvador, and I applied to work on the *Spectator,* but Charlie acted so snotty toward us, we decided we didn't want any part of it.

Besides that, the *Spectator* is a really lame paper. We knew we could do better and have more fun doing it too. We were right. *Zone* is the coolest.

Charlie zeroed in on me with her eyes. "There you are," she said. "I need to talk to you, Jessica."

I opened my mouth to say she had the wrong twin, but she didn't give me a chance to speak.

"I'm writing an article on Homecoming, and I need to know—how is everything going with the plans for the Homecoming dance?"

My mind raced. What should I do?

I could tell her she had the wrong twin and send her to find Jessica. That would be simple. For me. But not for Jess. She was totally stressed about this dance. She didn't need Charlie breathing down her neck about it too.

Jess wants me to help her, I thought. *So I will.*

"Things are really coming along," I told Charlie, trying to look confident.

She squinted at me. "Can you be more specific?"

"Well . . . no. Not really. I don't want to spoil all the big surprises we're planning." I didn't know what else to say. I didn't have a clue what

Jessica had already planned. (Or if they had planned anything at all.)

But I wasn't about to tell Charlie that.

"It sounds like you haven't made much progress," Charlie said suspiciously.

Okay, maybe Charlie is a pain, but you can't accuse her of being stupid. And she's not a bad reporter either.

"Oh no! We've accomplished a lot," I lied. "But there's still a lot more to do. It's a big job. But my committee and I are confident that the dance will be completely successful."

"How reassuring." Charlie smirked and jotted something down in her notebook.

What is she writing? I wondered desperately.

She looked up, and we stared at each other a moment. Then Charlie walked off without even saying good-bye.

I can't stand her! I was thrilled to have told her exactly what she *didn't* want to hear, even if it was a lie. But as I watched Charlie's retreating back, I wondered if I'd made things better for Jessica or even worse.

Jessica

"Hang your head over, hear the wind blow . . . ," I sang for about the fiftieth time. The bell had already rung and music should have been over, but Mrs. Roos was keeping us until the sopranos came in at just the right time and sang in harmony with the altos. It didn't seem like that was going to happen, though. We'd been struggling with the same song for the whole class and just couldn't seem to get it right.

My voice cracked all over the place. But I'm an alto, so all I had to do was plod along until the sopranos came in and ruined everything.

I looked at my watch. I was late for my dance-committee meeting. Not that I minded. I'd been dreading it all day.

I'd made some decisions since the last meeting, though. It was time for me to step up and really act like a leader.

I would give out the assignments and get everyone so busy working, they wouldn't have time to argue. I had to be firm with everyone. Well, everyone except Damon.

I couldn't imagine what he thought of me after the last two meetings. Especially after I'd shouted at everyone. He probably thought I was a bossy, loudmouthed freak.

But today I was going to blow him away. I'd blow everyone away.

"Hang your—" The sopranos joined the altos one note too soon.

Mrs. Roos clapped, and everyone stopped singing. "All right." She sighed, shaking her head. "I can see we're not going to get this right until next week. You're free to go."

I lunged for my backpack and headed out the door.

"Try singing to yourself as you're walking around," Mrs. Roos called after us. "It helps train your ear."

Yeah, right, I thought as I hurried toward my meeting. *That would really improve my social situation!*

I stood outside the cafeteria and took a deep breath. I could see my friends, sitting around a big, round table. This was it. I was going to be *firm*.

It didn't take more than two steps inside for me to understand that I was already in trouble.

My committee was once again doing what they seemed to do best.

Fighting!

Most of their backs were to me, and they obviously hadn't seen me coming.

"Listen, when Jessica isn't here, I'm kind of in charge," I heard Kristin say angrily.

Talk about bossy!

"Why?" Bethel demanded fiercely. "Is that one of your special executive powers as class president?"

"Hold on a minute." Ronald spoke up. "As locker partners, Jessica and I enjoy a special relationship. She counts on me for sound judgment. I think it's safe to assume that I am her intended second in command."

I couldn't believe my ears. Second in command? What was everyone talking about? Who had ever said anything about a second in command? It made me angry to hear them bickering again, but I had to keep my cool or I'd just make things worse.

"Oh, really, Ronald?" I demanded, stepping up to the table.

Everyone's heads whipped around. Ronald's face and neck turned red, and he stared down at his lap. He looked mortified.

"You guys are all fighting over who's in charge when I'm not around? Well, I'm here now—so let's get to work, okay?"

Silence. Good. My firmness was working.

"I hope you've all thought about what you want this dance to be like. I know I have. Most of all I want to make sure the music is great. I've been researching DJ's and I think Dr. Daddio is probably our best bet."

I took a deep breath. My so-called friends looked glassy-eyed. *Is any of this registering,* I wondered. "I think each of you should come up with the thing you most want to do for the dance and do it. We all have different opinions and tastes, but we want to appeal to everyone."

Ronald had returned to his normal color. He cleared his throat. "What about my fossil-dig idea? Or the gym being broken up into sevenths—"

Kristin let out an exasperated sigh, and Ronald stopped talking. I stared at her. Sure, Ronald's idea was lame and inappropriate, but she didn't have to be rude about it.

"What?" I demanded, raising my eyebrows at her. "Everyone can focus on one thing. If Ronald's really into the fossil dig, then . . . why not?"

"Oh, come on, Jessica." Kristin laughed. "You know it's lame. You don't have to be so nice all the time, you know. You can say what you think."

My mouth fell open, and a lump formed in my throat. Kristin, Ms. Popularity, always nice to everyone, was telling me how to act. And she wasn't being very nice about it. At all.

"Kristin," Brian said. He looked almost timid, like he was worried Kristin was going to say something mean to him now. "Jessica is just trying to be diplomatic."

"Oh, really? And you know all about that, don't you, Brian?" Kristin demanded, glaring at him. She was unstoppable!

Be firm, I reminded myself.

"That's okay, Brian. I can defend myself," I interjected. "So, Kristin. What would you like to work on?" I asked, putting on a fake, tour-guide smile.

"I don't know," Kristin said, crossing her arms and pouting like a four-year-old. "Ask Bethel."

"She just wants me to bring up the theme thing again," Bethel countered. "So she can complain about it."

"I do not!"

I looked across the table at Damon. He'd been so quiet. He had his chin on his hands and looked like he might be about to fall asleep. His eyes were fixed on something on the opposite wall of the cafeteria. I followed his gaze: the clock.

He wants to be here as much as I do, I thought. *Not at all!*

That's when I realized, I really *didn't* want to be there at all. Not with that crowd. I'd thought it would be a good idea to bring all my friends together, that we'd turn into this amazingly close group. Talk about the worst idea ever. They all hated each other, and when I thought about it, they weren't even very good friends anyway. I really didn't care if I ever saw any one of them again.

"Look, I don't think we're getting anywhere," Kristin started to say. "We're supposed to be planning a dance."

"What a joke!" I shouted, jumping to my feet. Hot, angry tears sprang to my eyes before I could stop them. "As if *any* of you have done *anything* to help with this dance at all!"

Damon sat up, and everyone stared at me blankly, as if I was the crazy one.

"Well, thanks a lot!" I knew my face was bright red. Plus my nose was dripping, tears were streaming down my cheeks, and I was trembling so much, it felt like my head might explode. Normally I would have been embarrassed to go off like that in front of Damon. But I was way too upset. "You know what? I don't care about the dance anymore. I'm out of here!" I shouted. Then I turned and ran out of the cafeteria.

I didn't care if I had to do detention for the rest of the year. There was no way I was planning the dance, not with those people.

I couldn't believe I'd thought for a single instant that I could count on any one of them.

Some friends they had turned out to be.

Kristin

I felt bad when Jessica ran out of our meeting in tears. I really did. But I couldn't bring myself to go after her.

Brian was shaking his head and looking at me like it was all my fault. Like he expected me to run after Jessica and apologize and bring her back. And that's why I couldn't do it. I couldn't prove him right. If anything, I was going to be the last one to leave. I mean, we had a dance to plan, right?

Damon stood up and looked at his watch.

"All right, guys," he said. "I gotta get home. I'll catch you later."

"See you later, man," Brian called in his best guys-unite! voice.

Thankfully, Damon didn't respond. He slung his backpack over one shoulder and headed for the door.

Bethel stood up and tossed a crumpled piece of paper on the table. "That's my idea for a decoration," she said to no one in particular. "You can use it if you want." Then she sort of stalked away.

I glanced at Brian and Ronald, as if daring them to go next.

Ronald had his hands spread out on the table and was lifting each one of his fingers in succession, as if he was counting.

Brian reached down for his bag and stood up. "Well, guess I'm taking off." He paused, looking down at me, as if he was waiting for me to say something. I glared back at him, he shrugged, and then he turned and walked away.

I stared at Ronald, still working his fingers. Finally they grew still, and Ronald's eyes met mine. "I guess a fossil dig wasn't such a great idea after all," he said.

I almost laughed, but Ronald looked so sad. He got up very slowly and gathered his notebook and pens together. "See you tomorrow, Kristin," he said, bobbing his head in my direction. Then he took off.

I watched Bethel's crumpled piece of paper, lying on the middle of the table, as if I was waiting for it to move. *Just leave it,* I told myself. *It looks like she's pretty much quit the committee anyway.* I stood up and grabbed my book bag off the back of the chair next to me. I was about to walk out of there when something made me lunge back and snatch up the piece of paper.

We needed all the ideas we could get. Especially if I was the only one left on Jessica's dance committee.

THE SPECTATOR
Our Homecoming Dance

Knock, knock
Who's there?
The Homecoming dance committee
Sorry, nobody's home.

Not funny? Maybe not. But nobody will be laughing if there's no one home Saturday after next, when students and friends plan to attend a big Homecoming dance here at SVJH.

Is there reason to worry? Not according to eighth-grader Jessica Wakefield, last-minute replacement as head of the Homecoming dance committee. "We've accomplished a lot, but there's a lot more to do. It's a big job. But we're confident that the dance will be completely successful," she says.

To this reporter, Wakefield's words are not very promising.

Do we detect a decided *lack* of confidence? It seems that by now Ms. Wakefield should have been more forthcoming with reports on a dance theme, colors, music, and much, much more.

The dance is a big event here at SVJH. Some might argue it is the biggest event. Perhaps a newcomer to our school doesn't fully appreciate the importance of the task she's been given or what a serious embarrassment it would be for alumni, teachers, and students (not to mention the dance-committee chairperson *herself*) to see a less than satisfactory effort. It's not too late to hand the reins of control over to a more experienced student. A ninth-grader, perhaps?

But that's just one reporter's opinion.

Charlie Roberts
Editor

Jessica

Dear Diary,

I wonder how much plastic surgery it takes to completely change a person's face. Because I need a total identity change. And some new friends.

I can't believe how my <u>so-called friends</u> have been acting. I guess I expected too much. They're all just selfish jerks.

At this point I don't think there's any way for me to save this dance. There's only one thing to do—step down from the committee. Of course, I'll probably get detention instead. Great. As if I don't already have enough problems.

All I wanted was to plan a really cool dance with all of my friends. Now I'm back where I started. Friendless Jessica Lamefield, the loser new girl.

Damon

"There's nothing more romantic than a dozen red roses," Sharon, fourteen, tells us. "Guys don't realize how a little trip to the florist can make such a huge difference."

"How much?" I asked the florist again. I couldn't believe how much a dozen roses cost!

Not that Jessica wasn't worth it. She definitely was. It's just that between buying the magazine and that nice gray T-shirt, my savings were shrinking fast.

There had to be something else I could buy her instead of roses.

I stared into the florist's case. Roses weren't right for Jessica anyway, I decided. They seemed too uptight and formal.

A bunch of daisies sat in a tall vase beside the roses. Now *those* were just right—cute, spunky, energetic.

"Um—I'd like to reserve a bunch of the daisies," I told the clerk behind the counter. "I need them by six o'clock the night of the junior high Homecoming dance."

She smiled and wrote down my order. "You're smart to order them now. We'll be very busy that evening."

I walked out of the florist's shop, feeling a little down. The perfect-Homecoming-date thing wasn't working out so well. I mean, instead of a new outfit I had a T-shirt. Instead of a dozen roses I had a bunch of daisies. Jessica was going to think I was completely lame.

And I hadn't even asked her to go with me yet.

Elizabeth

I knew the look on Jessica's face. I'd seen it a million times before. Forehead creased. Brows slightly down in the middle. Eyes narrowed and unblinking.

That's the Jessica-digging-in-her-heels-not-going-to-budge look of total stubbornness.

She'd started wearing it after her Monday dance committee meeting. Now it was Tuesday afternoon, and the look was still plastered on her face. I was worried it would stay like that forever—I had to do something.

"What's going on?" I asked, sitting down on the couch next to Jessica, who sat, arms crossed, staring at nothing.

"I've made a decision," she replied. "I can't run this dance. I might have to go back to doing detention—and it will look bad—but not as bad as if I totally mess up Homecoming for everyone. So I'm quitting my job as head of the dance committee. And I'm never speaking to any of my friends again."

75

Elizabeth

I felt my throat tighten as I remembered what I'd said to Charlie Roberts: *"We've accomplished a lot, but there's a lot more to do. It's a big job. But we're confident that the dance will be completely successful."*

I hadn't told Jessica about Charlie's interview. She never reads the *Spectator* anyway, and I didn't want to worry her even more.

But half the school had already read what I'd said—the *Spectator* came out on Tuesday after lunch. If Jessica gave up now, she'd look like a total liar!

"But Jessica!" I gulped. "You can't quit!"

She shook her head stubbornly. "No, Liz," she said. "It's over."

I could see she was serious. Which meant I had no choice. I had to tell her what I'd said to Charlie.

"Did you read the latest edition of the *Spectator*?" I asked anxiously.

She scowled even more deeply. "You know I don't read that thing. Why?"

I swallowed hard. Someone was bound to show it to her sooner or later. Sitting beside her, I dug in my backpack for the paper. I turned to Charlie's editorial and handed it to her.

Her eyes raced across the page. "That little creep!" she cried. "Where did she get this quote?

I never said this. I never even talked to her!"

"Um. I know you didn't. *I* did," I admitted.

"What?" Jessica stared at me.

"She thought I was you and started asking me about the dance," I explained. "I thought I could help by handling Charlie for you. I knew you didn't want to deal with her. It was the least I could do."

"But Elizabeth, if I step down now, everyone in school will think I'm a total fake!" Jessica moaned and flopped back on the sofa, her body limp. "How could you!"

I winced. I really had made things worse. Much worse. Poor Jessica. I stared at the purple butterfly patch on the knee of her jeans. It was just like the purple butterfly on my white summer nightgown. All of a sudden I had a great idea.

"Jessica," I said, excited that I'd discovered a way to help her. "I know what we can do!"

"What?" Jessica muttered, still lying there like all the air had gone out of her.

"A switch!"

She sat up, her eyebrows raised. "What?"

"You know," I explained patiently. "We've done it like a thousand times before at SVMS. We'll switch places."

Jessica still looked dumbfounded. "But—,"

she said, and stopped. "You hate switching. I always had to beg you to do it."

"I know," I admitted. She was right—I do hate it. "But I want to help."

"So *you* would plan the dance?" Jessica asked doubtfully.

"Sure," I said. "No problem. We'll switch clothes. No one ever has to know. Okay?"

"I don't know," Jessica said, gnawing a cuticle. "You hate dances."

"So? You can give me all your notes—I'll do it just the way you want it," I pleaded.

"Promise?"

"Promise," I assured her.

"Okay, I guess," Jessica agreed reluctantly. "It's not like I'll be going to the dance anyway."

I wasn't sure what I had just gotten myself into or if I should have let Jessica work a little harder to talk me out of it. But I was committed now.

"Don't worry," Jessica said. "I'll go to your *Zone* meetings—"

"No way!" I interrupted. "*Zone* is much too important to me."

I certainly wasn't going to let Jessica mess with *Zone*. She had absolutely no interest in it at all, and she wasn't exactly best friends with Salvador and Anna either.

"No matter what, *I'm* still going to my own *Zone* meetings," I insisted. "We'll just have to switch clothes before I go to your dance meetings. Then you can meet me in the bathroom on the second floor, and we'll switch back. Then I'll go work on the 'zine."

Jessica cocked her head as if she was trying to imagine if it would all work. Then her face broke into a smile, and she reached out to hug me.

"Oh, Liz! Thank you, thank you, thank you, thank you!" she exploded, looking happy, relieved, and grateful all at once. "You're the best twin sister anyone ever had! I'll give you all the lists I've made for the dance, and you can wear anything you want of mine. You're a lifesaver, Elizabeth. I love you."

She planted a big kiss on my cheek.

At least *she* was happy again.

That made one of us.

I had a sinking feeling that I'd just made one of the biggest mistakes of my short career at SVJH.

To: BigS1
From: wkfldE
Re: A strange request

Hi, Salvador.
   Listen, for the next few days I might seem a little weird to you. You know, kind of not myself. I can't explain why. Just don't take anything I say or do personally. I'll be back to normal after Homecoming.
                              Elizabeth
   P.S.: Tell Anna.

To: wkfldE
From: BigS1
Re: Your strange request

Dear Elizabeth,
   What's up? Are you in trouble? Are aliens doing experiments on your brain? Your secret is safe with me.
                              Salvador

To: BigS1
From: wkfldE
Re: Alien experiments

Hi again, Salvador.
   No, I haven't been abducted by aliens! It's just something I have to do to help a

friend. I just wanted you not to worry. I'll be back to my old self soon. And it won't affect the 'zine, I promise. Try to understand, and don't forget to tell Anna. Okay?
                    Elizabeth

To: wkfldE
From: BigS1
Re: I'm worried about you

Elizabeth,
  This is *muy misterioso!* Sure everything is all right?
                    Salvador

To: BigS1
From: wkfldE
Re: Don't worry

Salvador,
  Everything is *muy bueno*. Really. I think.
                    Elizabeth

Jessica

My twin sister, Elizabeth, is the absolute best!

We figured that the first thing she had to do was talk to the Homecoming dance committee members (pretending to be yours truly, of course), apologize for my outburst, and set up another meeting. She got to work right after we talked.

If anyone could fix this mess, I knew Elizabeth could. She always thinks before she speaks. She would never blow up like I had in our last meeting.

Not that any of this is really my fault. If my "friends" weren't being such *serious jerks* (except for Damon, maybe), I could have handled the dance just fine.

I am so mad at them!

But with Elizabeth on the case, I can actually hope that my social life at SVJH isn't completely over.

Right before lunch we traded clothes in the girls' room as kind of a test run. It was the first switch we'd ever done at Sweet Valley Junior

High, so we weren't sure how it would go over.

I stood in front of the mirror, trying to look serious and tucking my hair behind my ears. It wasn't used to being in a middle part and kept trying to escape. Beside me Elizabeth put her hands on her hips and stuck out her tongue at her reflection. I had to admit, my hot pink tank dress looked almost as good on her as it did on me.

"Wait a minute," I said as were about to walk out to the cafeteria. "Does this mean I have to eat lunch with Dork 1 and Dork 2?"

She shot me a look. "If you mean Salvador and Anna, then yes."

"Oh, do I *have* to?" I asked. Salvador is a total goofball, and Anna is just so—so *blah*.

"Jessica! I'm doing you a huge favor! The least you can do is hang with my friends so they don't think I'm blowing them off," Elizabeth insisted.

"All right," I grumbled. "But they're your best friends. Can't you just tell them about the switch?"

She shook her head. "They'd try to keep the secret, but you know how things get around. One of them could slip. Or someone might overhear them talking about it. And with Charlie Roberts poking her nose in everyone's business, it's better if you and I are the only ones who know."

"I guess you're right," I agreed.

We headed into the crowded cafeteria

together. As soon as we got there, Elizabeth spotted Kristin and hurried off to talk to her.

Good call, Liz, I thought.

But that left me standing alone, feeling amazingly weird.

What should I do next? What would *Elizabeth* do?

Think like Liz, I coached myself.

I saw Salvador and Anna sitting together at a table. *Like it or not, that's where you have to go.* I waved enthusiastically and carried over my lunch bag.

"Hi," Anna greeted me as I sat down.

I pulled out my sandwich and began to unwrap it. "Hi," I replied.

Salvador stared at me. Was that normal for him? I wasn't sure. But it was freaking me out. "What's new?" I asked him casually, hoping he would stop staring at me like a psycho.

"I finished my comic for this issue," he said. He slid a piece of paper across the table.

"Oh, great," I said, looking down at the paper.

Yikes! What on earth is this? I wondered. There was a drawing of some kid saying he was lost and couldn't find his home. In the last frame he bumped into a tree.

Huh?

"It's a student from Sweet Valley Junior High during Homecoming," Salvador explained. "Get it? *Homecoming.* It's a spoof of that editorial

Charlie Roberts wrote—the one about how there will be nothing to come home to if Jessica doesn't step things up with the dance plans."

I bit my lip. "Oh yeah, *that*," I said.

"So, do you want to use it?" Salvador asked me.

What did I know? Maybe Elizabeth's friends thought something like this was funny. "Sure," I said. "It's hilarious."

"Really?" Anna asked me, scrunching up her little button nose. "I didn't think it worked."

Oops! Wrong answer, apparently.

"No?" I asked. "Why not?"

"I just don't get it," she said. "I read the *Spec* article, but I didn't make the connection. Salvador had to explain it to me first."

"Oh, you're right," I agreed. Anna and Salvador were staring at me again like I was some rare species of weirdo.

"But you just said it was hilarious," Salvador objected.

"Uh . . ."

I felt like yelling, "Elizabeth, get over here!" But of course, I couldn't do that without blowing our whole plan.

"Um . . . at *first* I thought it was hilarious," I muttered. Then I had an idea. "I mean, not everyone read that *Spectator* article. So this comic thing has to, like, speak for itself, you know?"

Anna pulled at her superstraight black hair, still staring at me. Then she glanced down and studied the cartoon. "Why don't you add a panel?" she suggested.

"Yeah," Salvador agreed, getting excited. "I could add another panel where Jessica flies in, dressed as a superhero. Homecoming Girl or something."

Anna smiled. "Jessica could show the kid the way to the dance. Then the kid could say something like, 'Homecoming Girl saved the day! There is a Homecoming dance after all!'"

Lame idea, I thought. *The lamest. I can't believe we're even having this conversation.*

While Salvador and Anna continued to discuss the stupid comic strip, I glanced around the room for something—anything—more interesting to look at.

I spotted Elizabeth at a table talking to Ronald. (Poor Liz!)

I twisted around in my chair, coming face-to-face with Damon, walking up the aisle between the tables. He was about to go right past us.

"Hi, Damon!" I said brightly, and gave him a shy smile. He was the only member of my committee I was still willing to be civil to.

He glanced down at me and frowned in confusion. "Uh, hi," he said with a small wave, and kept on walking.

My shoulders drooped with disappointment.

He didn't even stop! He really must think I was the biggest jerk in the world for yelling at everyone at the meeting.

Then I remembered. He thought I was Elizabeth!

Damon and Elizabeth didn't know each other that well. He probably thought it was weird that I—I mean she—even said hi.

When I turned back around, Salvador was staring at me again. He looked kind of upset. Maybe it bothered him that I'd said hi to Damon. He's always had a crush on Elizabeth. Maybe he was jealous. *Ugh*.

"Do you think that would fix it?" he asked me. He shoved the cartoon at me again.

I bit into my sandwich and shrugged. I figured if my mouth was full, I didn't have to answer. I didn't want to say what I really thought about the cartoon. Elizabeth would never say anything unkind.

But Salvador just waited patiently, staring at me with his huge brown eyes while I chewed.

I took another big bite and stared back at him defiantly. For the first time in my life, I was dying for the bell to ring so I could finally get out of this hell that was lunch. But it's not like I had anyone better to eat with anyway. I mean, I'd pretty much discovered that I was absolutely friendless. That is, except for Elizabeth. And she was too busy *being* me to pay any attention to me.

The Homecoming Dance Committee

Wed., 1:19 P.M., study hall, Kristin's journal

Jessica came over to apologize for going ballistic at our last meeting. She really didn't have to. It was my fault too. I have been totally overreacting to Bethel. If Brian didn't always side with her, she might not bug me so much. But I guess I should just get over that.

Jessica suddenly seems so focused and calm! Maybe she started meditating or something. I've never really seen this side of her. I totally admire it. She seems really determined to get this dance going.

I think I'll just drop the school-colors issue. I won't even bring it up at the meeting. We need to start working together as a team, and the color scheme really doesn't matter that much anyway. And since I've decided I'm not talking to Brian anymore, I don't care if he sides with Bethel or not.

Wed., 1:19 P.M., study hall,
back page of Damon's notebook

Man, I am such a jerk. I must have done something totally wrong because Jessica is mad at me. Sure, she was polite and stuff when she came to talk to me about the dance during lunch. Way too polite! It was like we were complete strangers. (Meanwhile Elizabeth gave me this big hello. She probably feels sorry for me since she knows Jessica hates me now. They're pretty close, I think.) I feel like such an idiot. I made all these plans for the dance. There's no way she'll go with me now. Of course, I still haven't asked her yet.

Wed., 1:19 P.M., study hall, Bethel's journal

Jessica sure takes this dance stuff seriously. After the last meeting I was sure she'd quit. I know I was ready to. I guess Jessica is stronger than I thought. And you know, if she can tough it out, then so can I. Every time that know-it-all Kristin opens her mouth, I won't let her bother me. After all, it's only a dance, not a track meet. That's what Jessica said today. I thought it was a pretty good analogy.

And she's right. It's not like there are any winners here, so why not just play with the rest of the team?

Wed., 1:19 P.M., science lab, Ronald's laptop computer journal

She likes me. She really likes me! I knew it was only a matter of time before Jessica came around. Today at lunch she approached me about my ideas on the dance. She listened intently, and then she said she thought the idea of dividing the gym into sevens was both mathematically satisfying and conceptually unique.

Just before she left, Jessica said, "Ronald, I'm going to give these ideas a lot of thought, and we can discuss them at the meeting." Then she smiled. She didn't even glare at me once!

Wed., 1:19 P.M., library, Brian's journal

Kristin's been giving me the cold shoulder. I guess she's pretty mad at me about the school-colors thing. But I was only trying to be fair to Bethel. Just because Kristin and I are going out (pretty much) doesn't mean I'm supposed to agree with everything she says. Right?

Anyway, I'm glad Jessica hasn't totally given up on our dance committee. It gives me a chance to be with Kristin. Like Jessica said, we really need to work as a team. And that's exactly what I want to be with Kristin — a team.

Kristin

"Hey," I said when I entered the gym, not meeting anyone's gaze directly. Bethel was leaning against the wall near the door, like she was ready to bolt anytime. Brian and Damon were sprawled out on the floor. Damon was cleaning out his backpack, and Brian was kind of reading one of his comics, but not really. He was watching me—I could feel it. But I looked away, at Ronald. He was pacing the length of the gym, putting one foot carefully in front of the other. No one was talking.

"Hey," I said again, to no one in particular. "Where's Jess?"

Bethel shrugged, her eyes fixed on the red line taped across the middle of the gym floor.

Just then Elizabeth came in, dressed in Jessica's pink tank dress. She tucked her hair behind her ears and pressed her hands together in front of her like she was praying.

"Hello, everyone," she said. "Let's get started."

I stared back at her. Yes, it was definitely Elizabeth. What was she doing here?

Bethel

"About the issue of colors," Elizabeth said. She reached down and scratched her right knee. Yeah, I knew I wasn't crazy—it was definitely Elizabeth. Last week in track Jessica had tripped over a water bottle and bruised that knee on a piece of gravel. It was just a tiny purple bruise, but it wasn't anywhere to be seen on this girl's knee. Elizabeth's knee.

"Oh, you know, I've been thinking," Kristin cut in. "It doesn't really matter what colors the dance is decorated in. I mean, what's important is that it's a really good dance, right?"

Elizabeth glanced at me, her brow furrowed. I guess Jessica had filled her in, and she was worried I was going to leap down Kristin's throat. I had been pretty bad.

"Yeah," I conceded. "You're right."

Everyone stared at me as if they were waiting for the punch line. I shrugged back. A girl is allowed to change her mind.

"Well, we only have a little time left, so let's

concentrate on doing what we can. Let's make the place look nice, get good music and great food, and everyone will have fun," Elizabeth said brightly, clapping. She should try out for the cheerleading squad.

But no one could argue with her.

"I think Bethel has a good idea for a decoration." Kristin spoke up. My eyes were practically popping out of my head when she pulled out the piece of paper I'd almost thrown at her in the cafeteria. It was my idea for a big mural of the history of the SVJH football team.

"Good," Elizabeth said, beaming at me. "Why don't you two work on it together?"

I glanced at Kristin hesitantly. She was staring at the back of Elizabeth's head, but she caught my eye and made this really funny face, like, "What planet is *she* from?" I smiled. So Kristin had figured out that the girl pretending to be Jessica was really Elizabeth. It looked like sure Kristin wanted to talk, and the mural would be a good chance to do it. I mean, I was dying to figure out what was going on.

"I'll go get some paper from the art room," I volunteered.

Brian

Kristin was avoiding me. I kept trying to get her to look my way, but she was being pretty stubborn about it. Like, Brian's side of the gym: Whoa, off-limits! But then Jessica sent her and Bethel off to the corner to work on some big mural, so I gave up.

Jessica was acting pretty weird.

"So, guys," she said to me and Damon. She was all enthusiastic, like it was our first meeting. "Why don't you two make a list of all the food and drinks we'll want for the dance?"

"We'd better plan on getting a huge amount, with Ronald around," Damon joked.

I chuckled. But Jessica glanced over at Ronald, like she was worried his feelings might be hurt. Hello? Ronald just stood there, with his hands in his pockets, grinning his head off at Jessica. He sure wasn't the subtlest guy in the world.

"Yeah," I agreed, scrounging a piece of paper and a pencil from out of my bag. "And since we're going to need so much stuff, we'll probably both need to do the lifting and all that."

"Yeah," Damon agreed, punching me lightly on the arm. He was all right.

"Good," Jessica said cheerfully, as if it was all settled. "We can go over the list when you're done and see if we're sticking to budget. Now, Ronald, maybe you could help with the lights." I watched Jessica head over to Ronald, tucking her hair behind her ears and walking purposefully. Just like Elizabeth.

Wait a minute. It *was* Elizabeth! I was sure of it.

Huh?

I glanced over at Kristin, dying to ask her if she'd noticed. But her head was bent over a long sheet of brown mural paper, her back to me.

Damon

The minute she walked in, I knew
it wasn't really her. Sure, she looked like Jessica,
and she was wearing Jessica's cute pink dress, but
she didn't have that . . . Jessica-ish *thing* about her.
It was Elizabeth, pretending to be her. She was so
serious about it too that there was no way I could
just blow her cover and say, "So, Elizabeth, why
are you pretending to be your sister?" Besides, I
didn't really need to ask. We had all done such a
great job of bickering like little kids and not helping Jessica at all that I wouldn't be surprised if she
never wanted to talk to us again. The least we
could do was be cool to her sister. I looked over
Brian's shoulder at the list he was starting to make.

Pizza
Popcorn
Pretzels

"Hey, the three essential Ps," I joked.
Brian laughed and wrote down *Pepsi* and *Dr*

Pepper. "Five," he said. "Well, sort of. I mean, *Dr* is just a title."

"Pistachios," I said.

"Peanuts," Brian added.

"Potato chips," I muttered. I glanced up at Elizabeth. She was leaning over Ronald's laptop, pointing at the screen. Okay, so Jessica had asked her sister to fill in for her since we had been too much to take. But would Jessica still go to the dance with me? Or was she too mad?

Just then Elizabeth glanced up from the computer at the wall clock and her eyes nearly popped out of her head. She jumped up, whirled around, and headed for the door. "You're all doing great! Keep it up!" she shouted, running out into the hall. "I'll talk to you all tomorrow!"

"Yeah, I gotta get going," Brian said, standing up. He chucked his pencil at me. "We're late for our *Zone* meeting."

We? Did he mean him and Elizabeth? "So you noticed?" I said, raising my eyebrows at him.

"How could I not?" Brian asked.

I glanced over at Bethel and Kristin. Bethel was looking up at Brian, nodding. Kristin just looked worried. I guess everyone had pretty much guessed that wasn't Jessica.

The question was, how were we going to get Jessica back?

Elizabeth

Go! Go! Go! I chanted silently as I raced down the hall. I could *not* miss this *Zone* meeting.

I wasn't going to let Jessica fill in for me either. At lunch I'd glanced over and seen Salvador staring at her like she was some kind of freak. I don't know what they were talking about, but I kind of wished I could have listened in. I bet it was pretty hilarious.

I wanted to tell Anna and Salvador what was going on. I knew I could trust them with the secret. But I didn't want to risk any unintentional slipups. If the wrong people found out about the switch, Jessica could get in a lot of trouble. I mean, this whole dance-committee thing was supposed to be a punishment. Mr. Todd wouldn't like it if he found out she wasn't really running the meetings anymore.

I was almost to the girls' room when Jessica popped her head out the door. "Hurry up! Hurry up!" she called.

"Get inside," I snapped at her. Nervously I glanced around to make sure no one had spotted us. No. The hall was empty.

I flung open the door and met Jessica inside. She was dressed in my favorite blue plaid skirt and long-sleeved white T-shirt. She had my denim jacket in her hands. She shoved it at me.

"Don't undress out here," I objected. "Someone might come in. We'd better get into booths and pass the clothes underneath."

"Oh, okay," Jessica agreed. "How did my meeting go anyway?"

"Great," I told her. "No one suspects a thing, and a lot is getting done."

"Excellent," she cheered, twirling around in my skirt.

She was in midtwirl when the bathroom door flew open.

"Anna!" we both gasped at the same time.

She smiled at me, obviously thinking I was Jessica, then turned to Jessica. "Oh, there you are, Elizabeth," she said. "Come on, the meeting's already started."

Anna grabbed hold of Jessica's arm and began to steer her out of the girls' room.

Jessica looked over her shoulder at me for help.

Elizabeth

What could I do? I couldn't think of anything that wouldn't give away our switch.

I tossed my jacket to Jessica, and she caught it as Anna pulled her out into the hall.

"Oh no!" I cried, staring at my reflection in the bathroom mirror. Even I was almost fooled. I looked just like Jessica when she was about to cry.

Jessica

Considering what a shrimp she is, Anna had an amazingly tight grip. I felt like a little field mouse being carried away by an owl.

"You can let me go now," I suggested as she dragged me down the hall.

Anna laughed. "Oh, sorry."

The moment she released me, I wanted to bolt. After all, what's the use of being on the track team if you can't ditch a little pest like Anna Wang?

But I couldn't. I owed it to Elizabeth to suffer through this *Zone* meeting.

I don't understand why my sister and her nerdy pals can't just write for the *Spectator,* like normal people.

Actually, *Zone* is okay, I guess. I don't know. I've never really read the *Spectator.* But Elizabeth and her friends act like all of Sweet Valley will go up in flames if they don't have their meetings or meet their deadlines. They take it way too seriously.

Jessica

Now I was going to have to look like I took it really seriously too.

Anna and I reached the classroom just as Brian hurried down the hall toward us. "Good. You guys are late too," he said, panting. "I had to do that dance-committee thing. It looks like we're finally getting it together. Jessica's making sure it's going to be a really cool dance."

"Jessica is really organized," I said, trying hard not to smile too wide. Might as well give myself some good press.

"Jessica? Organized?" Anna demanded, like what I said was completely off base.

"Yes," I replied. "Very."

"She sure hides it well," Anna remarked.

Thanks a lot, I thought.

"Sorry. I know she's your twin and all," Anna added.

She must have noticed my annoyed expression. Actually, I wanted to slap her.

"Hey, come on, you guys," Salvador called from inside the classroom. "Let's get this issue done."

I went in and sat down next to Salvador. I hoped he was done with his dumb cartoon. If I had to try to pretend I knew what *that* was about again, I might lose my mind.

"I finished the article you assigned me," Brian

102

said, passing us each a copy. "You know, the one we talked about."

I glanced down at mine, and my breath caught in my throat. It was all about my favorite topic—me! Maybe this meeting wasn't going to be so boring after all!

STUDENT DETAINED FOR KILLING DOLPHINS
By Brian Rainey

In a horrifying turn of events, Jessica Wakefield (grade eight) was dragged to the principal's office last week by biology teacher Ms. Fenton. Her crime? Inciting the killing of dolphins.

Where did she find these dolphins?

Redwood Middle School.

As most of us know, the Redwood Dolphins is the team that will be battling our own Sweet Valley Junior High Wildcats at the big Homecoming game next week.

When Jessica wrote the slogan Kill the Dolphins on her spirited team poster, she was speaking figuratively of defeating the team, not of killing the seafaring mammal we all know and love.

Of course, Ms. Fenton is a science teacher, not an English teacher, and the environment is the subject most dear to her heart. But how many people will be sanctioned in the future if Ms. F. continues her particular style of environmental protection? Consider reading the following headlines in your newspaper:

PLAYER JAILED FOR TROUNCING ST. LOUIS CARDINALS
CHICAGO BULLS SLAUGHTERED—OPPONENTS ARRESTED
FULL INVESTIGATION ON BEATEN FLORIDA MARLINS

Jessica

I was laughing so hard, I could barely catch my breath. I wasn't surprised that Brian wrote it. He had a great sense of humor, unlike the other two drones at *Zone*.

"So, I guess you like it?" Brian said, grinning.

"It's awesome," I replied earnestly. I mean, considering the subject matter alone, it was a good article. But I also liked the style it was written in—sharp but with a fun side, not too dry.

"Maybe we'd better not mock Ms. Fenton so much," Anna worried. "Do you think we'll get into trouble? She's not exactly known for her great sense of humor."

Neither are you, I thought, annoyed. The part about Ms. Fenton was funny. I didn't want it taken out.

"Fenton only teaches seventh-grade bio," Salvador pointed out. "We won't have her ever again."

"Besides, what could happen?" I said. "I

105

didn't even really get into trouble. I just became head of the . . ."

I let my voice trail off. For a moment I'd forgotten I was supposed to be Elizabeth.

They all stared at me, but I was sure none of them had caught on.

"I became head of the . . . Jessica fan club," I finished. "I mean, I always knew Jessica was really brave and together, but after the way she handled *that* situation, I was blown away. Now I'm her biggest admirer."

Salvador squinted at me skeptically. "Since when?" he demanded.

"What do you mean?" I asked innocently. "Don't I always say nice things about Jessica?"

"Nice things, yes," he agreed. "But head of her fan club?"

"Well, you know what I mean," I said, brushing him off.

"No, not really," he replied.

"Well, figure it out!" I snapped, losing my patience.

He shrugged. "Anyway, this article rocks, Brian. I wouldn't change anything."

"I think it's great too, but maybe you need a little more about Jessica here," I suggested, pointing at the end of the article.

"What else about Jessica could we possibly

say?" Anna asked. From her exasperated expression I could tell she wasn't too hot on the idea.

"I don't know," I said, scratching my head and trying to act thoughtful, like Elizabeth would. "We could write about how Jessica got into the mess in the first place because she was so full of school spirit that she volunteered to make posters. And how she's serving out her punishment, being head of the dance committee, with such devotion."

"That's true," Brian agreed.

I smiled at him. Brian had been a pain in my dance-committee meetings, but he was still a cool guy. Kristin was lucky.

"Yeah," I went on. "She's doing a terrific job. And you could quote her saying how much she *adores* dolphins. I don't actually remember saying that—I mean, I don't remember *her* saying that, but it's okay. I'm sure she won't mind if I speak for her."

Salvador folded his arms and stared at me with those dark eyes of his. "How do you know she'd want to be quoted on something she didn't even say?" he asked. "That's bad journalism."

I laughed lightly. "We're twins. Of course I know."

"You look alike, but that's about it," Salvador commented.

"Don't underestimate the twin connection," I told him.

I meant it too. Elizabeth and I don't have to be alike to be superclose. It's something non-twins have trouble understanding.

"Come on, let's vote on this article," Anna said. "Does it go in as is, or does it need changes? I still think the Ms. Fenton thing should be softened up a little."

"Coward," Salvador teased her. "I think it's great the way it is."

Anna stuck out her tongue at him.

"You're the tiebreaker, Liz," Brian said to me.

"I still say you need more information on Jessica. This story could inspire kids. She's a real rebel here, a trendsetter," I enthused.

"Rebel?" Salvador sputtered, laughing.

I felt my cheeks grow hot and concentrated on being Elizabeth. *Don't snap,* I reminded myself.

"Trendsetter?" Salvador demanded.

"Yes!" I insisted. "She tricked the system. She didn't let Principal Todd stick her with boring old detention. Instead she showed us that there's an alternative. She's doing a great job as dance-committee leader. And no dolphins were harmed."

Salvador exploded with laughter. He grabbed his sides and nearly fell off his chair. "No dolphins were harmed!" he gasped through his laughter. "No dolphins were harmed! Oh, man. That's funny!"

"What?" I demanded. "It's true. They weren't."

He started laughing even harder, and Brian joined in, shaking up and down as he began to giggle uncontrollably.

I glanced at Anna. She stared back at me, one black eyebrow raised in disbelief.

What? I wondered. *What did I say?*

Brian calmed himself down and picked up a copy of his article. "Okay, I'll make some quick changes."

"Very quick," Anna said. "We have to get this issue out by the end of next week."

Salvador was still panting with laughter. "How about we meet tomorrow to start doing layout? Same time. Same place," he managed to say.

"You mean we're done?" I asked eagerly. Thank goodness. Between Anna's staring and Salvador's freaky laughter, I couldn't wait to get out of there.

And I was going to make sure *Elizabeth* made it to the next meeting. No matter what. I couldn't do this again, that's for sure.

I was already near the door when Salvador called out, "Bye, Elizabeth." Then he broke into another cackling fit. What a weirdo.

Kristin

"Are you sure?" Ronald asked.

"Yeah, come on, Ronald. Did you smell her?" Damon insisted.

"What?" Ronald cried, about to rush to Jessica's defense.

"She smelled like raspberries. Jessica always smells, um . . ." Damon blushed, looking flustered. But he soldiered on. "Jessica always smells sort of like peaches. She told me once that *Elizabeth* likes that raspberry bath stuff and she likes peach."

I wasn't aware that Jessica and Damon had had such intimate conversations. I bet Jessica would be pretty excited if she could hear Damon going on about what bath gel she uses. I had to say, it *was* pretty cute. I would have to tell her all about it. That is, if she ever spoke to me again.

"So? Maybe Jessica tried her sister's bath gel for the day. You don't have any factual proof that that wasn't Jessica," Ronald insisted. His fists were clenched, and I could tell that even he didn't really believe in what he was saying. He was probably just excited that Jessica (or Elizabeth—however you want to look at it) had been so nice to him.

Damon shook his gorgeous head. "Nah. It was Elizabeth. Think about it," he insisted.

All the way home I did think about it, and the more I thought, the more upset I got.

We'd let Jessica down, big time. Except for that last meeting we'd spent more time bickering than we had planning. And I was the worst of the bunch! I'd been so wrapped up in my status with Brian and my ongoing clash with Bethel that I'd barely given the dance any thought at all.

If I were Jessica, I probably would have quit the committee completely.

Then again, there was no way she could quit after Charlie Roberts's awful editorial in the *Spectator*. It would look way too bad.

All of a sudden I felt so, so terrible.

I mean, some friends we were—especially me! No wonder Jessica had gone into hiding.

Sure, we'd gotten our acts together today, but that didn't do Jessica any good. As far as she was concerned, she'd failed. And her friends were complete jerks.

We had to make this up to her. But how?

I walked inside my apartment door, tossed my backpack on the floor, and dropped onto the living-room couch. Mom wasn't home yet, so I had some privacy to make phone calls.

Reaching for the thick Sweet Valley phone book, I looked up *Rheece* and dialed Ronald's number. His mother answered.

"Ronald, it's a *girl*—for you!" I heard her say excitedly.

There was a dull thwack, as if Mrs. Rheece had dropped the receiver on the floor. Then Ronald answered with a falsely deep, "Hello."

"Hi, Ronald, it's Kristin," I said. "I'm calling about the meeting today." (I wanted to get that established fast so he wouldn't get his hopes up that I was calling to ask him out or something.) "Listen. You know what Damon said—about how it wasn't Jessica at the meeting?"

"I think sniffing people is an extremely rude habit," Ronald answered.

I smiled. Only Ronald would say something like that.

"But you know he was right," I said. "And we've got to do something to make it up to her."

Ronald was silent a moment. "Actually, he *was* right," he said. "Jessica has been far too nice to me lately. Normally she rolls her eyes or glares at me at least once a meeting. And that didn't happen at all today."

I knew Jessica tried to be nice to Ronald, but she didn't always find it easy. Actually, she never found it easy. He got on her nerves. And usually it showed.

"Ronald." I sighed. "I think we messed up. We were all so caught up in our own little worlds, we didn't help Jessica at all. And that *Spec* article dissing the dance committee certainly didn't help. Jessica's reputation is on the line, and it's up to us to deal!"

"That's true," Ronald agreed. "We must, er—*deal*. But how?"

"Well, actually it's kind of obvious. We have to make this the absolute best dance SVJH has ever seen. It's the perfect way to make it up to her. We have to give a hundred and ten percent—can you do that, Ronald?"

"Of course!" he said. "Where do I start?"

"Well, no offense. But does it really matter that the square footage of the gym is divisible by seven?" I asked, hoping my bluntness wouldn't offend him. "Let's just focus on the basics, like Elizabeth said today—music, food, drinks, lighting."

"Of course," Ronald agreed.

"No dinoland either," I insisted.

"No dinoland," Ronald promised.

He could be pretty cool once you got beyond the laptop and mathematical terminology.

"Thanks," I told him. "Way to go."

"But what do we say to Elizabeth?" Ronald asked. "That we want the real Jessica back?"

"Actually, I don't think we should."

"Why not?" Ronald asked, obviously surprised.

"Let's just get the dance planned and make sure Jessica is there to see how great it is. Okay?"

"Sure," Ronald agreed. "No problem."

"See you at our meeting tomorrow?"

"Yes!" Ronald exclaimed. He seemed to be getting more and more excited. "See you tomorrow!"

I laughed as I hung up the phone. Ronald was an oddball, but he was a *sweet* oddball. And he obviously cared a lot about Jessica. We had that in common.

The next person I had to call was Bethel. We'd gotten along fine making that football mural today. But we hadn't exactly talked. We'd just started painting and stayed out of each other's way.

Actually, talking was going to be a little harder. But I had to go through with it for Jessica.

I looked up Bethel's number and dialed. The phone rang once, but then my call-waiting tone came on and I clicked over.

"Hello?" I said.

"Hey. It's Bethel."

Bethel

"That's so funny," Kristin said. She actually sounded happy to hear from me. "I was just calling *you*. I was wondering what you thought about what Damon said—that Jessica, you know . . . was really Elizabeth," she babbled on.

"Well," I said. "I don't think there's that much to think about."

"Oh," Kristin said.

Cold. Definitely cold.

"Okay, well," Kristin continued. "I was just calling to try to be, you know, friendly. But—I guess not. So, um . . . I'll see you at the meeting tomorrow. Bye."

"Wait, Kristin—" I stopped her. "Listen, *I* called *you*. And I wanted to talk about what we're going to do, you know, to make it up to Jessica."

Kristin was silent, and I wondered if she'd already hung up.

"Hello?"

115

Kristin sighed. "Look, Bethel. I don't have anything against you. It's just that we both have strong opinions. Strong, *opposite* opinions. And ever since the election I kind of feel this major tension every time you walk into the room."

"I know what you mean," I told her. "I feel exactly the same way."

Kristin giggled and sighed noisily into the phone. "Actually, I'm sure I wouldn't have been such a jerk about it if Brian wasn't there."

"Brian? What does he have to do with it?" I asked.

"I—uh—I kind of like him as more than a friend. And I'm not sure if the feeling is mutual," Kristin answered.

"Yeah?" I responded, confused. "I thought you guys were already going out."

"No. We're not. I don't even know if he likes me anymore. And I know it sounds kind of stupid, but I wanted Brian to side with me about the colors. I guess I sort of lost it when he took your side."

"I get it," I said. "But I think he really does like you. More than you think."

"You do?" Kristin asked.

"Yeah, definitely," I said. "You should see the way he looks at you."

"Really?" Kristin asked. She sounded thrilled. "Hey, thanks, Bethel."

"Sure. No problem," I responded. "So, what are we going to do about this whole Jessica situation?"

Kristin started chattering on about how we all had to get together and make this the best dance in SVJH history.

After I hung up, I felt *so* much better. Yesterday if someone had even mentioned Kristin's name, I would have cringed. Now I'd definitely go up and talk to her if I saw her in the hall. It's kind of crazy how you can change your mind about a person so quickly.

Damon

The phone rang, and of course my little sister Sally ran to get it.

"Damon is eating yellow Jell-O," she announced into the receiver. "Yuck." Then she giggled, staring up at me with her silly big blue eyes.

"Gimme the phone, you goofy little cookie monster," I said, and bent down to tickle her. I could hear a girl laughing on the other end.

I froze. Jessica?

"Hello? Hello?" the girl was saying.

I snatched the receiver out of Sally's hand.

"Hello," I said. "Jessica?"

"Hi, Damon. No. It's Kristin."

"Oh. Hey," I said, trying not to sound bummed.

I cradled the phone with my shoulder, reached down, and picked Sally up by her ankles. Then I started swinging her back and forth. It's her favorite thing. Someday I expect to go into her room and find her sleeping like that. Like a bat.

"So," Kristin said. "I've talked to everyone else on the committee. Well, almost everyone. Well,

Ronald and Bethel. Anyway, we all agree that the only reason Jessica got her sister to switch with her is she just couldn't deal with us anymore. I mean, we were pretty hard to take, you know?"

I had to hand it to Kristin. She could sure make a speech when she wanted to.

"Yeah?" I said.

"Yeah. And so I just wanted to say that what we have to do is make this the most incredible dance ever. For Jessica, you know?"

"Right," I agreed.

"So at the meeting tomorrow, do everything Elizabeth, I mean, Jessica—you know what I mean—tells us to do and don't let on, okay? We want the dance to be kind of like a surprise for Jessica."

"Sure. I'll see you there," I said.

"Right," Kristin said. "See you."

I started to hang up, holding my sister's ankles in one hand.

"Hey, Damon?" I heard Kristin call, just as I was about to put down the receiver.

"Yeah?" I asked, putting it to my ear.

"Two things," Kristin said. Man, she liked to talk! "First, do you mind calling Brian to tell him all this? I've been on the phone for a while, and my mom really hates it when I tie up the line."

"Sure. No problem."

"And also. Um. I think you could really make

this dance special for Jessica. Do you know what I mean?" Kristin asked.

My heart started to beat a little faster. Kristin had no idea that I'd been stressing over how to make the Homecoming dance special for Jessica for the last two weeks!

"Yeah," I said. "Sorta."

"Good," Kristin said. "Okay. So I'll see you tomorrow. And don't forget to call Brian."

"Don't worry," I said. "Bye."

I lowered Sally gently to the floor. She lay there like a banana peel, waiting for the blood to go out of her head. I headed into my room to find that stupid magazine article again.

Alison, fifteen, tells us about the ultimate dance move: "You're dancing, and he's holding you close, and he leans in and whispers something totally romantic in your ear. Now, that's what really turns a date from nice into incredible!"

I tossed the article aside. Whisper something into Jessica's ear?

I pictured the scene. The school gym. Me, dancing with Jessica. I'm wearing my new gray T-shirt and holding her close. I lean in. My lips move close to her ear, and I whisper—

What?

Unsent E-mails from Brian and Kristin

To: KGrl99
From: BRainE
Re: Us

Dear Kristin,
   I know I haven't been the best boyfriend in the world, but I wish you would at least talk to me. I wanted to know if you would go to the dance with me. But now I feel sort of stupid asking. I wish we could just make up and hang out again like we used to.

To: BRainE
From: KGrl99
Re: Us

Dear Brian,
   I thought I knew you better. I thought you liked me. But now I can see that all those times we were hanging out and when you kissed me, you were just using me. All this time I was wondering when you were going to ask me out. Now I know the answer—never.

Elizabeth

When I arrived at the gym on Saturday, my whole committee—I mean, *Jessica's* whole committee—was already there, working, even though the dance was still a week away!

Kristin and Bethel were talking with the DJ they'd hired, Dr. Daddio. They sat on the bleachers, matching the CDs Dr. D. had in his collection with their list of requests.

Everything looked under control there.

Ronald was at another table, intently untangling lines of tiny, sparkling white lights to string around the doorways and the refreshments table.

Brian stood on a ladder, hanging up the big posters Kristin's poster committee had made. Damon stood at the foot of the ladder, patiently handing the posters up to him.

I watched as Brian came down, pushed the ladder over to the next spot, then stepped aside so Damon could climb the ladder. Then Brian handed up another poster and a box of tacks.

"Hey, Jessica," Brian called, waving.

Did I imagine it, or did he say "my" name in a funny way? No, I decided. There was no way he could know. Jessica had even picked my outfit this morning—cropped, boot-cut black pants and an aqua T-shirt with a shiny dragonfly on it.

I wasn't exactly comfortable in this outfit. The shirt was tighter than I liked. And the flared pants weren't really my style. But I definitely looked like Jessica. It was almost scary.

"What do you think of the decorations?" Brian asked when I walked up.

"Cool," I said, trying to impersonate Jessica as best I could.

"They're pretty good," Damon commented, studying the wall with a critical expression. "But Bri and I want to come up with something more. Something different."

Bri? I thought. Everyone was getting along so well, they were using each other's nicknames? Was I in the right room?

"When we think of something, we'll run it by you," Brian assured me. "Don't worry, Jess. Damon and I are on it."

"Excellent," I said, shocked but pleased.

Bethel walked over, smiling happily. "Kristin and I are going shopping tomorrow for paper tablecloths and napkins and stuff. All right?"

Elizabeth

"Kristin and you?" I asked, amazed. "Shopping—like—*together?*"

"Yeah, she and I are cool now," she told me.

"Great," I said, truly amazed.

I went over to Ronald. "Do we have enough lights?" I asked.

"No, but I took a little trip to Vito's Pizza. I recalled they strung this sort of light out front during the holidays last year. They were more than willing to let us borrow what they have. In fact, they're delivering them within the hour."

"You arranged all that?" I asked, impressed.

"Yes. Bethel and I talked about it first, though. She and I worked together to measure out exactly how much more footage of lighting was required."

I was starting to suspect that this was all a dream. An insane dream. A good dream.

But none of this could possibly be real.

"Ow!" Damon shouted, and dropped the box of tacks from the top of the ladder. "Damn."

"Watch it, buddy," Brian called up to him. "Those things have points."

They both laughed.

I tugged at my T-shirt. It kept riding up above the waistband of my pants.

Okay, so this wasn't a dream. My clothes were too uncomfortable for me to be wearing my cozy pj's, curled up under my fluffy down comforter, fast asleep.

This was real.

Ronald was still studying his strings of lights. "These are nice," he commented, "but I think we could do better. Do you mind if I talk to Mr. Bertram? I remember he had some blue lights he used in a play last year. If we paired those with these white ones, it would create an impressive effect."

"Sure. Go for it," I agreed.

"Jessica," Kristin called over to me. I walked over to where she sat with Bethel and Dr. Daddio at the bottom of the bleachers. "Dr. D. wants an hour for dinner break," she told me.

I glanced at the Doctor. He had beads in his beard and was wearing a wraparound skirt over his jeans. He nodded at me. "Union rules."

"But don't worry—we have a great plan we're working on to fill in the gap," Kristin added.

"We do?" I asked. "What?"

"Well, we'd rather keep it secret. I'm sure everyone will like it, though," she said, her eyes all lit up with enthusiasm.

"Wow. Okay," I agreed. I trusted Kristin—after all, she was the class president.

This was amazing! Everything was done or getting done.

I could think of only one thing left to handle—making flyers and tacking them up around school. But that was easy enough. I could take care of that by myself.

"Wow," I said again, surveying the gym.

Kristin put her arm around me. "Things are really coming together, aren't they, Jess?" she asked.

"Uh . . . yeah," I replied, suddenly feeling a little uneasy. Now Kristin was saying my name in a weird way. Wasn't she?

Or maybe Jessica's clothes were beginning to rub off on me. *She* was the paranoid twin, not me.

Damon

Jessica, your eyes are like pools of water.
No.

Jessica, you are really cool.
Uh—no.

Jessica, you smell great.
No way.

Jessica, I really, really _____ you.

_____?

I'd thought about it all last night
and all day Saturday, but I *still* didn't know what
great romantic thing to say to Jessica while we
were dancing.

Everything I came up with seemed either in-
credibly stupid or way too . . . slimy. I didn't
want her to think I was a complete dork. I
needed something cool. Casual, yet sophisticated.
With oomph, but not too much oomph.

Damon

But I was a blank. And I had a feeling I was going to stay that way.

Maybe I should just forget about the dance. I mean, I hadn't even asked Jessica to go with me yet!

I was running out of time.

Where *was* Jessica anyway?

Jessica

I was sitting on my bedroom floor, painting my toenails blue. It was weird knowing that at that moment, Elizabeth was running my dance-committee meeting—pretending to be me—and no one suspected a thing.

I so totally owed her. That's why I decided I was going to let her go to the dance—as me. Sure, technically "Jessica" would still get all the credit. But my sister had to get credit for all the hard work she'd done.

I could still go as Elizabeth. But honestly, how much fun would that be?

The phone rang once. A few seconds later Steven appeared in my open bedroom doorway, holding the cordless phone. "Is Liz around?" he asked. "It's for her."

"That depends," I said, carefully drawing the tiny brush over my pinky toenail. "Who is it?"

"It's Anna," he said impatiently.

"Give it to me," I commanded, and reached out to take the phone.

Steven tossed it to me, and I had to sort of lunge to catch it. My right foot smashed into my left leg, smearing blue polish all over it.

"Steven!" I shouted. But he was already down the hall.

I pressed the phone against my cheek. "Hi, Anna," I said in my most Elizabethan voice—sweet and earnest.

"Hi," Anna replied. "So my mom said she'd take us to the mall."

Hello? Had Elizabeth made plans without telling me?

"I know it's earlier than we said, but she can only take us now, so it's now or never. How fast can you be ready?" she asked me.

"Uhhhh . . ." I hesitated, looking down at my smeared toes. "I have sort of a headache," I said. Maybe it wasn't true then, but if I had to go to the mall with Anna, I was pretty sure I'd have one soon enough.

"So take something for it," she said. Her compassion was overwhelming. "I know you want to be in on this. After all, it was your idea."

Elizabeth! I complained silently. "Tell me the idea again," I said.

Anna sighed deeply. "Elizabeth, is this you?" she asked.

"Of course it's me! Who else would it be?"

130

"Jessica," she answered bluntly.

"Jessica has a dance-committee meeting," I insisted. "It's definitely me, and I definitely want to do the mall thing. I can be ready in ten minutes."

"Okay, Mom will drive Salvador and me to your house. She'll honk for you. Be ready."

Ugh! Not El Salvador too!

"Okay, great," I said, trying to sound upbeat. "I'll be outside the minute you honk."

Clicking off, I wobbled over to my dresser for nail-polish remover. My toes were a mess anyway. They'd never be dry in ten minutes. And sandals were out because blue toenails would be a dead giveaway that I wasn't Elizabeth. I had no choice but to wipe them clean. A whole half hour's work wasted.

When my toes were all cleaned up, I hurried through the bathroom to Elizabeth's room to put on her clothes. Ick. I pulled on a pair of straight-legged jeans and a plain red T-shirt. I tied a navy blue sweatshirt around my waist and then stepped into her blue canvas sneakers.

I inspected myself in the mirror. Whoops! My cute iridescent butterfly headband was still in my hair. I pulled it off and stuck my hair behind my ears.

I checked out my reflection once more. *Bo*ring, but definitely Elizabeth.

Jessica

About two seconds later a horn honked outside. I hurried downstairs, passing Steven, who was sitting on the couch, gabbing on the phone. "Tell Mom I went to the Red Bird Mall," I shouted as I headed for the door.

He shot me a confused look. "Wait a minute," he called. "Is that you, Liz? Jessica?"

I didn't bother to answer. If my own brother couldn't tell I was me, it was a good sign.

I hurried to the car. *Remember, you like Anna and Salvador,* I coached myself, trying to get into the Elizabeth state of mind. I slipped into the backseat with Salvador.

"Hi, Mrs. Wang," I said to Anna's mother in the front seat.

"Hello, Elizabeth," she replied as she pulled out of our driveway.

Salvador and Anna were staring at me again. I wondered if they were always this weird or if maybe they suspected something. How would I know? The only thing to do was be super-Elizabeth to dispel any suspicions they might have.

"This is so exciting, isn't it?" I said, faking as much enthusiasm as I could manage.

"What part of it do you like best?" Salvador asked.

"The mall part," I answered. It was the only part I knew about. "Going to the mall today was the best idea."

"That's funny," Salvador said in a teasing way. "It was *your* idea."

I smiled sweetly. "Of course. And it was a *good* idea."

"I think the stores will be glad to let you put *Zone* out on the counters," Anna's mother said.

So that was it! That was Elizabeth's big plan. Thank you, Mrs. Wang!

"If we split up, we should be able to cover the mall pretty fast," Anna suggested.

"I don't know," Mrs. Wang objected. "For safety's sake I'd like you three to stick together."

"Mom, *please!*" Anna said through gritted teeth. She was so intense.

"How about if we meet somewhere every twenty minutes?" Salvador said. "That way we can see how we're doing as we go along."

"That sounds good," Anna agreed. "*Okay*, Mom?"

"Okay," her mother agreed, not sounding very happy about it.

I sighed with relief. At least I could ditch these two as soon as we got there. I could browse around my favorite stores and only be bothered with them every twenty minutes. That wouldn't be too bad.

Anna's mother dropped us off out front, and we made our way into the mall. "I'll go upstairs and to the right!" I volunteered first. I wanted dibs on

133

the cool stores like AB/CD's and Fashion Train.

"Okay," Salvador said, handing me a stack of *Zone*s. "See you by the fountain in twenty."

I headed straight for Fashion Train. I *love* their clothes.

At the counter I asked if we could drop off *Zone* every issue. "The manager will be back in five minutes—can you wait?" the salesgirl asked.

"No problem," I answered.

Yes! Now I even had a reason to hang out and check out the clothes.

The first rack I went to had these adorable wrap dresses. They were sleeveless and tied under the right arm. I picked out a light blue one. Over the light blue was a sheer layer of fabric with dark blue flowers. Stepping in front of a mirror, I held it up. So cute! And it made my eyes look extra blue.

I sighed. It was exactly the kind of dress I'd pick out for the Homecoming dance. That is, if I was going.

I scowled at my reflection. The dress looked totally wrong with my dull Elizabeth hair.

I slid the dress back onto the rack and prowled around the rest of the store. But as I did, I began missing someone very much.

Me!

I was dying to get back to being Jessica. As far as I

was concerned, the sooner this whole Homecoming was over, the better.

"Oh, Kristin, you know I hate the way I look in pink!"

I ducked behind a rack of pedal pushers. It was Lacey Frells, with Kristin. Lacey hated me. It would be just like her to see right through my lame jeans and boring T-shirt and recognize me. I held my breath. What should I do?

Kristin held up a red peasant dress with tiny flowers embroidered all over it and a cute drawstring tie on the neckline. "What about this?" she asked. Lacey snatched the dress out of her hand and headed to the back of the store, where the changing rooms are. Kristin followed her, giggling. "If it's too big on you, I'm trying it!"

I crept out from behind the rack of pedal pushers. The woman behind the counter waved me over. "The manager won't be back for a little while longer. Can I have your number so I can let you know about your 'zine?"

"That's all right," I said, heading for the door so I could make my escape. "I'll come back some other time."

Countdown to the Big Dance

10. *(Sunday)* Kristin calls Lacey Frells. Begs Lacey to talk local band, Splendora, into performing at the Homecoming dance during Dr. Daddio's one-hour break. Lacey asks how much the school is paying. Kristin explains that they're not paying anything but begs Lacey to tell the band how many new fans they'll have if they do a free performance.

9. *(Sunday)* The band agrees to perform.

8. *(Monday)* Before track practice Bethel chases after Jessica (assuming she's really Elizabeth) to tell her to tell Coach Krebs she can't make it today—she promised Kristin she'd go shopping for supplies for the dance. Jessica sprints away before Bethel can catch up to her. Bethel watches her run and realizes it's the real Jessica she was chasing.

7. *(Monday)* Kristin and Bethel go to Vito's to discuss how much of a deposit they need to put down on the pizzas. Ethel, Vito's wife, offers to throw in subs and sodas free of charge. "Since you girls are so cute together."

   Since they now have extra money to spend, Kristin suggests buying a huge cake for dessert. Bethel insists most people like ice cream better. They argue for thirty seconds, then buy a huge ice cream cake instead.

6. (*Tuesday*) Mr. Bertram, the English teacher, helps Ronald install theatrical lights in the gym. One of Mr. Bertram's former students, now an engineering student at SVU, comes in to visit Mr. Bertram. He and Ronald begin to discuss the dance, and he offers to install a light-and-laser show he invented for an SVU party. Ronald accepts the offer immediately.

5. (*Wednesday* A.M.) Elizabeth prints out the fantastic flyers she's created on her computer on neon paper and hangs them all over school.

4. (*Wednesday* P.M.) Brian sees Jessica in the hallway on the way to history. "Hey, great flyers, Jess," he says, walking next to her. Jessica turns bright red and heads for the girls' room.

3. (*Thursday*) Brian and Damon work in Brian's yard to build a ten-foot wildcat from cardboard, plywood, and papier-mâché. Damon retrieves his four-year-old sister's tiger doll from his backpack and tucks it under the

wildcat's arm, like a baby wildcat. The toy tiger is movement activated and growls when you get near it.

2. *(Friday A.M.)* Damon sees Jessica (dressed as Elizabeth) eating lunch by herself in the cafeteria, pretending to read a book. He contemplates sitting down with her, then changes his mind and heads outside to eat his sandwich on the school steps.

1. *(Friday P.M.)* By eight o'clock everything in the gym is in place. Elizabeth (dressed in Jessica's bright blue overalls) commends everyone for a job well done. She leaves with a happy wave, promising to see everyone at the dance the next night.

0. *(Friday P.M.)* When Elizabeth leaves, the committee members stand around, wondering if they've really thought of everything. "This is awesome, isn't it?" Kristin says, gazing at their crazy decorations vaguely undulating beneath Ronald's laser-light show.

"I can't wait until the *real* Jessica sees it," Bethel adds. "She's coming, isn't she?"

Everyone glances at each other. No one knows for sure.

Kristin

I should have been in a great mood on Saturday. The dance was going to be beyond awesome. And I had a great surprise planned for Jessica.

But instead I felt totally grumpy. The reason why wasn't a big mystery either. It was Brian. We hadn't spoken two words to each other all week.

I'd had such big dreams of the two of us dancing together at Homecoming. And now that wasn't going to happen for sure.

I headed for the refrigerator, looking for a snack. What I really needed right then was some chocolate. While I stared into our nearly empty fridge, the phone rang. I scooped it up, still staring.

"Hello?"

"Hey. It's me," Brian's familiar voice came on the other end.

Whoa! My heart instantly started to pound.

"Hi," I said hesitantly. *Why is he calling?* I wondered, my mind racing. *To apologize? To ask me out?*

"Damon just called me," he began. "He said you had some plan for tonight."

"Yeah?" I said.

"Well, how are we supposed to help if we don't know what the plan is?"

Not an apology. But . . . okay. I guessed it was about time I told everyone what I was up to. I just didn't want anyone to spill the beans so it would get back to Jessica.

"Here's what I've been thinking," I explained. "Jessica probably isn't going to show her face at the dance because she's mad at all of us and because she probably thinks it's not going to be that great anyway. So I say we all go over to her house and *make* her come to the dance with us. I was even thinking of making a sign like a formal invite to the dance that said, We're Sorry, Jessica, or something like that, at the end of it too. Does that sound okay?"

"Uh. Sure," Brian agreed. "I guess."

"Okay, then," I said. "Let's all meet in front of Jessica's house about a half hour before the dance."

Of course I had envisioned Brian and me walking to the dance together, all dressed up and glowing with adoration for each other. But that, clearly, was not going to happen.

"Okay," Brian agreed. He was being so quiet!

"See you then," I answered, feeling disappointed.

Until now I hadn't really *believed* that Brian didn't like me at all. But it was sure starting to sound that way. I clutched the phone, about to slam it back into the cradle on the kitchen wall.

"Uh . . . Kristin?" Brian said.

"What?"

"I wanted to ask you one more thing," he said quickly. "Do you think that maybe . . . for, like, the first dance . . . we could . . . um . . . dance together?"

Yes!

"Sure. I mean, you know, we'll see how it goes," I answered casually.

"Oh. Okay. Great. See ya." He hung up.

I hung up.

Well, he didn't exactly ask me to the dance. But I'd already told him we were all going to-gether, so he didn't really have any choice. Asking me to dance was the next best thing.

Brian is actually kind of sweet.

This dance was going to be awesome!

That is, if we could manage to drag Jessica there. I had a feeling it was going to be harder than it sounded.

The Sweet Valley Junior High

Homecoming Dance Committee

would love the pleasure of your

company at tonight's festivities.

We're sorry, Jessica!

Elizabeth

"Are you sure you want me to wear this?" I asked Jessica. "You've only worn it once before."

She'd loaned me a long, straight, dark gray sheath dress with spaghetti straps and tiny light gray flowers beaded all over it. A shiny, metallic gray cardigan went over it.

It would have looked great on Jessica, but it was totally not me. In fact, I wasn't really that keen on going to the dance at all.

"Why don't you just go yourself, Jess?" I asked. "Really. Everything is done. Just go and have a good time. It's going to be great—and you can take all the credit."

"No way!" Jessica cried from her bed, where she was lounging around in her pajamas. "You did the work. *You* take the credit!"

"But everyone thinks you planned the party anyway," I pointed out.

"Yeah, but you should be there to see how much fun everyone has and hear everyone say how great it is," she argued.

143

Elizabeth

I sighed. "Honestly, Jess, I didn't really do that much. Your committee did all the work. I really don't see why you're making me go to a dance I don't even want to go to."

Jessica crossed her arms in front of her. "Well, sorry. There's no way *I'm* going. And it would look kind of strange if the chairperson didn't show up for her own dance, wouldn't it?"

I stared back at her, shaking my head. She certainly didn't look like a person who was even *considering* going to a dance. She had no makeup on and was wearing a sweatshirt and boxer shorts covered in red hearts. Her hair was piled on her head and bunched up in a scrunchie, the ends jutting out in all directions.

"I know what you need." She hopped off the bed, dug around at the bottom of her closet, and pulled out a pair of strappy black platform shoes.

"No way. I'll break my ankle in those," I protested.

"Any other kind of shoe will look dorky with that dress," she insisted. "What were you planning to wear—loafers?"

I had opened my mouth to argue when the front doorbell rang.

"It's probably for Steven," Jessica said.

But then our brother yelled up the stairs, "Jessica, your little Homecoming crew is here!"

Jessica and I locked eyes. What where *they* doing here? "You'd better see what they want," Jessica said, holding out the platforms to me.

I ignored the shoes and hurried to the stairs. "Hi," I said when I saw the group standing at the bottom of the stairway.

"Hi," Damon said, looking me up and down. He climbed toward me, a bunch of daisies clutched in his fist. I was starting to feel a little jittery. Damon looked nice, but I didn't want to pretend to be his date all night! The rest of the group followed him up the stairs.

"How come you guys are here?" I asked.

But they stepped past me without answering. Kristin led them to Jessica's door.

"Wh-Where are you going?" I asked, hurrying after them.

Kristin turned back to me. "We want you to come to the dance, Elizabeth," she said. "But we want Jessica there too."

I sucked in my breath. Oh no! They knew!

Jessica

"Hi, Jessica," a soft, deep voice said. I glanced up. Damon was standing in my doorway, looking more amazing than he ever had before. He strode toward me, carrying a bunch of flowers.

Was I imagining this?

I jumped up, standing on my bed as if he were a mouse in my room. I looked like an idiot in my heart-print boxers, but it was too late—there was nothing I could do.

Bethel, Ronald, Brian, and Kristin charged in after him. Kristin and Brian were holding up a big, handmade sign inviting me to the dance. "What's going on?" I cried, staring at the sign and then back at my friends.

"Jess," Kristin said, shaking her curls—she looked gorgeous, in the red dress from Fashion Train and strappy cream-colored sandals. "We were such jerks, and we are *so* sorry. We kept you from planning the dance. But it's going to be okay now—we finally pulled it

together. Anyway, we want you to forgive us—
and come have fun."

"Come on, Jessica," Bethel urged. "I'm
going—you have to go!"

"But I—I'm Elizabeth," I protested weakly,
sinking down on my bed. Where had Liz and I
gone wrong?

"*Sure,* you are," Brian said with a laugh. "You
can stop playing around now. You had us tricked
for a minute. But we're on to you, Wakefield."

My mind spun. How long had they known? And
why hadn't they said anything about it until now?

I didn't know how to feel. I guess I was glad.
My friends had come to get me. They'd made
that adorable sign. And they were apologizing.
Best of all, they knew me well enough to know
that I was really me.

"You never fooled me," Ronald insisted. "You
have this thing you do with your eyes whenever
I annoy you too much. Elizabeth never did it."

"And she doesn't smell like peaches either,"
Damon added softly, in a way that almost made
me melt. He looked at me with his soft, blue eyes
and handed me the bunch of flowers in his hand.

Daisies! I stared at them, stunned. How did
Damon know they were my favorite flower?

"You *have to* see the band this girl got to play
during the DJ breaks in the party," Bethel added,

slapping Kristin's shoulder. "And Dr. Daddio really rocks."

"We have a *band*?" I asked.

Kristin grinned at Bethel. "And wait till you see the food. We all worked on it together, but Bethel is the one who thought of ice cream."

Hello? Talk about shock. Bethel and Kristin were . . . getting along?

"And if you don't come, you'll never see the light show Ronald got together," Brian added.

"*Light show?*" I exclaimed, staring at Ronald. "Liz—how did you pull all this off?" I asked.

She shrugged. "I told you; I didn't really do much. These guys did it all."

"We had to make it up to you somehow," Bethel said, as if it was no big deal.

My throat tightened, and I felt tears welling up in my eyes. I hadn't even realized what amazing friends I'd made at my new school. They totally cared. It was such a relief.

"Come on, Jess, let's *all* go," Elizabeth said.

"Well." I cocked my head and laughed. "It sort of depends—would you mind if I wear that dress?"

"It's yours," Elizabeth agreed, smiling. "As long as you promise to wear the platforms too."

"Okay." I leaped down from the bed. "Now, everybody out," I commanded. "I have to change!"

Kristin

My dream was coming true after all.
Jessica was there somewhere, and I was wrapped in Brian's arms, swaying to a slow song as a rainbow of colored lights cascaded over us.

What could be more romantic?

"I'm glad you're not mad at me anymore," Brian said softly, still moving to the music.

"I just thought that . . . well . . . it doesn't matter," I replied. It was true. I could barely remember what I'd been angry about.

Brian squeezed me a little tighter, enough to make me believe he liked me as much as I liked him. I rested my cheek, ever so slightly, on his shoulder.

When the song ended, we stopped dancing and stood close, our hands brushing against each other. The flashing lights stopped, and the bright ceiling lights came on. We turned to see Principal Todd pick up Dr. Daddio's handheld microphone.

"This is one of the finest Homecoming dances

I can recall. I would like to praise Jessica Wakefield and her committee for pulling together this fabulous event. Jessica, could you come up here, please?"

The room exploded with applause. Jessica—the real Jessica—strode toward the mike, never once wobbling on her platforms. She was smiling, her eyes shining. She looked amazing.

The principal handed her the microphone.

"Thanks," Jessica said. "But really the thanks goes to my committee, who are the absolute best."

She named all of our names, and every one of us got a round of applause. "I'd also like to thank my sister, Elizabeth, who had a bigger role in this than anyone knew." Brian nudged me, and I laughed as everyone applauded.

Then the music started up again, and Brian reached for my hand. I glanced up at him.

"Don't just assume you can dance every dance with me without asking," I told him.

"I thought boyfriends and girlfriends always danced together," he said, swaying from foot to foot to the music. He looked kind of goofy. In an adorable way.

"Boyfriends and girlfriends?" I demanded, feeling my heart race.

"Yeah. I thought that's what we were," Brian insisted, still swaying.

"Since when?"

"Since always. Since we kissed!"

"Really? You did?"

"Yeah. Didn't you?"

"No," I answered, looking down at the toes of my sandals. I could feel my face getting hot. "I thought you'd *ask* me or something. You know, to make it official."

"Oh," Brian said. He stopped swaying and shoved his hands in his pockets.

"Oh, what?" I demanded.

Brian took his hands out of his pockets and rested them on my shoulders. He looked into my eyes, his face completely serious. "Kristin, will you go out with me?" he asked.

I smiled up at him and began to sway to the music. "Shut up and dance," I answered.

Jessica

Another slow song came on when Dr. Daddio got the mike back. I was walking toward the drink table, looking for Bethel, when someone tapped me on the shoulder. It was Damon.

I couldn't believe how gorgeous he looked. I'd never seen him so dressed up. He was wearing black jeans and a nice gray T-shirt (it really brought out his eyes), with a black button-down shirt over it.

Not too far from his usual style. Just a little—nicer.

I couldn't believe the bouquet of daisies he'd given me either. I'd never have guessed Damon could be so romantic. Or even that he liked me that much!

He held out his hand and led me out onto the dance floor.

He put his hands lightly on my waist. I reached up and rested my hands on his shoulders. We started to dance.

"I can't believe it," I said softly. "This dance

has gone from being the worst nightmare to one of the best ever. I mean . . ." I looked up into Damon's deep blue eyes and blushed.

Damon leaned over and brushed his lips against my cheek.

I could feel my face burning up. But I didn't care. He kissed me!

Then he moved his lips close to my ear.

"Jessica," he whispered. "*You* are the best ever."

My breath caught in my chest. I pressed my head into Damon's soft gray T-shirt. I couldn't look at him—I was blushing too much. But I was sure it was okay.

I closed my eyes. His T-shirt was *so* soft.